Lost on the Bayou

Rose Pressey

Copyright © 2014 by Rose Pressey

All rights reserved, including the right to reproduce this book or portions thereof in any form, (electronic, mechanical, photocopying, recording, or otherwise) without the prior written permission of the copyright owner.

This book is a work of fiction. The names, characters, incidents, places, and brands are the product of the author's imagination and not to be construed as real. The author acknowledges the trademarked status and trademark owners of various products referenced in this work of fiction, which have been used without permission. The publication/use of these trademarks is not authorized, associated with, or sponsored by the trademark owners.

PRAISE FOR ME AND MY GHOULFRIENDS BY ROSE PRESSEY

"Rose Pressey spins a delightful tale with misfits and romance that makes me cheer loudly."
—*Coffee Time Romance*

"Her characters are alive and full of quick witted charm and will make you laugh. The plot twists keep you turning the pages non-stop."
—*ParaNormalRomance*

"I absolutely loved this book! It had me chuckling from the beginning."
—*Fallen Angel Reviews*

ROSE PRESSEY'S COMPLETE BOOKSHELF

Maggie, P.I. Mystery Series:
Book 1 – Crime Wave
Book – Murder is a Beach

The Halloween LaVeau Series:
Book 1 – Forever Charmed
Book 2 – Charmed Again
Book 3 – Third Time's a Charm

The Hadley Wilds Series:
Book 1: Dead Girl's Guide to Style

The Rylie Cruz Series:
Book 1 – How to Date a Werewolf
Book 2 – How to Date a Vampire
Book 3 – How to Date a Demon

The Larue Donovan Series:
Book 1 – Me and My Ghoulfriends
Book 2 – Ghouls Night Out
Book 3 – The Ghoul Next Door

The Mystic Café Series:
Book 1 – No Shoes, No Shirt, No Spells
Book 2 – Pies and Potions

The Veronica Mason Series:
Book 1 – Rock 'n' Roll is Undead

A Trash to Treasure Crafting Mystery:
Book 1 – Murder at Honeysuckle Hotel
Book 2 – Honeysuckle Homicide

The Haunted Renovation Mystery Series:
Book 1 – Flip that Haunted House
Book 2 – The Haunted Fixer Upper

DEDICATION

This is to you and you know who you are.

ACKNOWLEDGMENTS

To my son, who brings me joy every single day. To my mother, who introduced me to the love of books. To my husband, who encourages me and always has faith in me. A huge thank you to my editor, Eleanor Boyall. And to the readers who make writing fun.

CHAPTER ONE

Chloe used to believe in happily ever after

"Abby moaned beneath her breath. Matthew settled his mouth on her lips." I typed the sentence and then finished with the words "The End." Leaning back in my chair, I released a deep breath and blew the bangs out of my eyes and stared at the computer screen. One day and two hours before my latest deadline and I'd finished the manuscript. All that was left now was to send it to my editor. I deserved a high-calorie, buttercream-frosting-topped treat after all the work I'd put into this book. The story had been emotionally draining and I'd gone along for every twist and turn of the passionate ride with my characters.

With a click of the mouse I attached the file to the email and hit send. The manuscript was on its way. My editor would be happy that I'd met the deadline since I was pretty sure she'd expected it to be late for the second time. I'd asked for an extra month to write the book. My head just hadn't been in the right place lately. Maybe I needed a vacation.

Too bad my romance novels were nothing like my life. Sometimes I wondered how I ever wrote the love scenes since I had no passion headed my way. I didn't even have anyone to flirt with at the moment, not even a wink.

Unless you considered Mr. Henkel who lived next door. He had an eye twitch that most people mistook as a wink.

Heck, maybe lack of romance made my imagination even better. I hadn't had a date for six months. Sure, I'd been asked out, but what was the point? It never ended in a happily ever after.

The sun melted through my apartment window, covering the room in a buttery yellow glow. I had been so busy in my made-up world the last few weeks that I'd let the real one pass me by. I watched as a few people walked past. Maybe it was time that I joined them.

I pushed to my feet and then walked over to the bookshelf at the far corner of the room. My apartment had one bedroom and a living-dining room combination. The windows in each room stretched from ceiling to floor and allowed in an abundant amount of light. With light-colored walls, aged white furniture, and wisps of white fabric, the décor of my place brought forth feelings of romance and passion. I had quite a few novels lining my shelves since I'd first been published eight years ago. I had been lucky enough to start a great career as an author. Since I was only thirty-three, I still had many novels left to write.

I picked up one of the paperbacks. The name Chloe Beaumont was splashed across the spine. It was still strange seeing my name on my books. I never tired of it though. I placed the book back on the shelf and crossed the floor over to the window. The people who had been walking by had now disappeared. With the window open, only the sound of a bird filled the air. Palm trees and cactus bushes dotted the landscape. Beyond them was the complex parking lot.

My apartment was in a small complex with only twenty other units. As far as I knew I was the youngest resident. Most everyone was in their seventies and spent their days playing golf or reading books by the pool. Then again, I didn't really know any of my neighbors other than Mr.

Henkel who lived right across the hall. He made sure that I knew he was around too. I think he'd decided early on that he needed to be a father figure for me. I didn't have the heart to tell him that gesture wasn't necessary. After all, it was kind of sweet that he'd cared.

I'd moved to Arizona ten years ago after college. My father had remarried and moved to New York. My mother had died my senior year of high school. I didn't see a need to stay around town. There were too many painful memories and nothing good for me in Belle Grove, Louisiana.

The men in my novels were my idea of perfect. Sure, they had their flaws, but who didn't? Why couldn't I meet someone like that in real life? Because they didn't exist in real life. It wasn't that I didn't believe in the happily ever after, but I had to admit I was a bit skeptical now. I had never actually met anyone who could be compared to a hero in one of my novels—well, there was one person who I'd thought was the ideal guy, but he'd turned out to be the exact opposite. I'd just kept writing my idea of the perfect man and that would have to be enough.

A knock on my door startled me out of my reverie. I peeked out the little hole in the door and saw Mr. Henkel looking back. He didn't know that I was watching him just yet. Most of his gray hair had disappeared years ago. He wore his usual outfit of short-sleeved button-down shirt and plaid shorts. Mr. Henkel was a fan of wearing white socks with his sandals.

I opened the door. "Good morning, Mr. Henkel, how are you?"

"Just thought I would check and see if you'd like anything from the store. I'm getting oranges. Would you like an orange?" He adjusted the wire glasses on his face and peered at me.

Just then my phone rang. "Oh, I'd better get that, Mr. Henkel. I don't think I need any oranges today."

His face broke into a smile, crinkling the corners of his eyes. "I'll see you when I get back then."

I reached my phone and paused when I saw the caller ID. It wasn't the number that made me pause. No, the reason I stopped was the location listed. It was my hometown. Who was calling me from there? My uncle still lived there, but I hadn't talked with him in a while. Plus, it wasn't his number, although maybe he was using a different phone. There was only one way to find out. "Hello?"

I had fully expected to hear his loud voice boom across the line. It wasn't his voice though. In fact it wasn't a man's voice at all. A soft woman's voice sounded from the other end.

"Is this Chloe Beaumont?" she asked.

I hesitated, but then finally said, "Yes, this is Chloe."

"I'm sorry for calling. My name is Gina DeWitt."

Where had I heard that name before? I waited for her to continue.

"I'm your Uncle Taylor's girlfriend."

Oh, yes, now I remembered. He had mentioned that he was dating someone. "What can I do for you?" I asked.

"Have you spoken with your uncle lately?" Her voice wavered.

I hadn't talked with him. Heck, I didn't even know how she'd gotten my phone number. Had he given it to her? Maybe they were planning on getting married. I hoped not, because I didn't want to be invited to the wedding. That would mean going back to Belle Grove and that wasn't something I was willing to do.

I didn't know much about her other than what my uncle had said over the phone. She worked at the local bakery. He went in every morning for a coffee and a bagel. After a while, I guessed they'd started talking and now apparently they were an item. She was my uncle's age—well, maybe a couple years younger, around fifty-six. He said she was a petite blonde with a bubbly personality. I had to admit I wasn't sensing that bubbly personality right now. Maybe she was mad at him. But why call me?

"So you haven't talked with your uncle?" she pressed.

"No, I haven't spoken with him in a while. Is everything okay?" I asked. She was beginning to freak me out.

She released a deep breath and then said, "I have a bit of a problem."

Well, I had figured that much since she was practically a stranger and calling me to discuss my uncle. I thought I detected tears in her voice. "What's wrong?" I asked, hoping that she would get to the point.

"I can't find your uncle," she said matter-of-factly.

"What do you mean you can't find him?" My voice was now squeakier than usual.

"I haven't seen him in three days and that's just not like him."

"Did you try to call?" It seemed like an obvious question, but I had to ask.

"Yes, of course I've tried to call him," she said in an irritated voice.

"Sorry, but I had to ask the obvious questions. Did you go by his place?"

She sighed. "Yes, of course."

"Maybe he just decided to take a little trip," I offered.

What did she want me to do? He was a big boy and maybe he didn't want to talk with her. Maybe they had had a fight. But what if they hadn't? My stomach twisted at the thought. What would I do? I had to call him as soon as I hung up with her. Surely he would answer my call.

My uncle had always been a free spirit, but now that he was older he had settled down. He liked to stay close to home and go fishing a couple times a week. When he wasn't working, he liked to take it easy. "What had he been doing?" I asked.

"He was busy trying to get things together to build his new house," she offered.

Uncle Taylor had mentioned he was going to build his dream home on some land that he'd had for a while. I was glad that he was finally making that dream come true. The perfect spot, as he'd called it, was on the water, where he could do what he loved best, fishing.

"We had a bit of a disagreement when we spoke last." She sniffled. "Now I regret that."

So maybe it was an argument that had caused this. Trouble in paradise. "What was the argument about?"

"Oh, Taylor didn't want me to come along when he was meeting some man. I know the jerk and don't like him, so I didn't want him to go. He would harass me anytime I saw him out in town," she said.

What? That was a detail she should have mentioned earlier. "Have you contacted the man he was supposed to meet?" I asked.

"No, I didn't want to talk to him." She paused, and then said, "He's not very nice."

Well, that was a problem.

"Will you come here and help me?" she asked.

My stomach sank. My worst fear had just come true. The thing I wanted to do the least. I'd rather run around the neighborhood naked than go back to Belle Grove.

With desperation in my voice, I asked, "Have you contacted the police?"

"Yes, they said that there's nothing they can do." There was a hitch in her voice and then she continued, "He's an adult and they didn't suspect any foul play."

Well, it looked as if I had no choice.

"Please. I know how much he adored you." The sweetness flowed like a chocolate fountain.

He did? He'd never told me that. What choice did I have? I would have to go back to Belle Grove.

She pleaded again and it appeared that I had no choice but answer now.

Looking around the room, I realized I would have to leave the safe haven of my home. I released a deep breath. "Yes, I'll be there as soon as I can get a flight."

She sighed. "Thank you so much."

I jotted down her number and promised to call her as soon as I arrived. In the meantime, I dialed my uncle's number and prayed that he would answer. Unfortunately, it went straight to his voicemail. I hung up the phone and ran my hand through my hair. How had this happened? As much as I didn't want to go back, there was something more important… I had to find my uncle. My mother would have wanted it that way.

I'd just started packing my suitcase when a knock sounded on my door again. I rushed over and saw Mr. Henkel again. When I opened the door, Mr. Henkel thrust an orange at me.

"I brought you an orange anyway. You look like you need the extra calories." He gestured with the fruit.

"Thank you, Mr. Henkel." I took the orange from his outstretched hand. "I'm glad you stopped by. I'm going to be away for a few days."

"Oh, really?" His eyebrow lifted. "Where are you headed?"

"I'm going back to Louisiana for a short trip."

He shifted the grocery bag on his arm. "Beautiful part of the country. Don't worry, I'll keep an eye on your place."

"Thank you," I said.

"Don't forget to eat the orange." He waved his bony finger.

I held up the orange. "I promise."

I finished shoving clothes into my bag and hoisted the suitcase onto the floor. Thank goodness the thing had wheels. I'd have to pick up insect repellent when I got to Louisiana. The weather would be a lot different there. Hot and humid was something I hadn't thought about in a long time, but there were a lot of things about Belle Grove that I hadn't thought about in a long time. Things that I had tried to push to the back of my mind.

After grabbing my purse and locking the door, I headed for the parking lot. I'd take a cab to the airport. Within a short time, I would be in Baton Rouge. I'd decided to rent a car and drive from there.

I forced myself to purchase the plane ticket and check my luggage. Once I boarded my flight, it was too late to turn back. Soon I was surrounded by clouds and well on my way back. I'd find my uncle and get out of Belle Grove as soon as possible.

CHAPTER TWO

Grant never expected to see Chloe again

There was just enough time for me to grab lunch before I had to be back at work. I pulled up in front of Belle Grove's best diner, Fancy Diner. The food wasn't particularly good, but the burgers were thick and juicy and sometimes the waitresses gave me a free slice of pie.

The sweltering heat had a tight grip on the afternoon air, as if the sun was angry at us. I was looking forward to the cool air in the restaurant. Too bad I didn't have time to eat it there. I had to be back at the office within twenty minutes, so I'd have to grab my food and run.

I climbed out from behind the wheel of my brand-new shiny black Ford F-150 and had just rounded the side when I spotted her.

I stopped in my tracks. I couldn't believe my eyes. What was she doing back in Belle Grove? Was it really her? I looked closer. She hadn't noticed me. But yes, I was positive that it was her.

As far as I knew, she hadn't been back in town for over ten years. I'd kept track, but I wouldn't share that info with anyone. The guys at work were always on me because I didn't have a woman in my life. Not to mention my mother talked about it every time I saw her. I'd had a few girlfriends, but nothing had ever worked out. Now Chloe was back.

She hadn't changed at all and she looked great, with the same smokin' body and gorgeous shiny dark hair. The smell of strawberries came rushing back. Chloe had always smelled like strawberries and sweet whipped cream. Her big brown eyes and the way her mouth twisted to one side when she smiled drove me crazy. Was she back in town to stay or just passing through? I knew her Uncle Taylor was still in Belle Grove. But according to him, she never came around or called often. When she'd left years ago she hadn't looked back.

Would she remember me? How could she forget? We'd dated the last year of high school and then through college. I'd screwed up when she'd thought I'd cheated on her.

Her car looked like a rental, so maybe she wasn't here to stay. Chloe was parked across the street at the bank's parking lot. I watched as she got out of the car and walked back to the car's trunk. She lifted a suitcase out of the trunk. That had to mean she was going to stay for a while.

Just then the thing opened and dumped her clothing all over the ground. If I remembered Chloe, I knew she was probably cursing under her breath as she picked the items up from the pavement. She shoved the items back into the suitcase and dumped it into the trunk. Surprisingly, she hadn't noticed that I was staring.

I felt guilty standing there just watching her. Should I have gone over and volunteered to help pick up the clothing? She probably would have just turned me away and told me to get lost. I wasn't ready to take that chance. What would I have said? Long time no see? That sounded kind of lame. This was an awkward situation and I'd never been good with awkward situations. I would just have to wing it and see what happened though. If Chloe told me to get lost then I'd walk away as if nothing had happened.

I stepped toward the back of the car and waited as a couple of cars drove by.

I'd just stepped off the curb when someone called out my name from behind me. I turned around and saw my brother Ty standing behind me. People thought we were twins with the same dark hair and eyes. He was an inch shorter than me, although he never admitted it.

"Hey, what's up?" he asked.

"I was just getting lunch." I motioned toward the diner, avoiding looking at Chloe.

Did I look guilty? What did I have to be guilty about? I was only going over to help her out. But no doubt he would give me a hard time for that. Maybe he wouldn't notice Chloe. No way. Her beauty would stand out in any crowd. He looked at me with a suspicious eye and then glanced over my shoulder. Too late. He would see her now.

"I recognize that look. You look guilty of something." He crossed his arms in front of his chest.

"You don't recognize anything." I looked over my shoulder. She was gone. How had she gotten away so quickly? Had she noticed us? I bet she'd heard him call out my name. No, there was too much noise from traffic for that. At least that was what I told myself.

"What are you doing here?" I tried to change the subject.

"I came to see Mom and Dad." He eyed me intently.

I nodded. "Yeah, okay. Tell them I'll stop by soon. I need to get my lunch and head back."

He still stared at me with that suspicious look. "You look as if you've seen a ghost," he said.

I felt like I had seen a ghost. It didn't look as if he was going to let me off the hook with this one. I'd have no choice but bring back a topic that I'd thought had died a long time ago. It was funny how this town had a way of dragging things back that should have been dead and buried a long time ago.

His stare was focused on me like a hawk and I couldn't believe that he wouldn't just mind his own business. He'd always been that way though, always trying to fix everyone's problems.

I leaned against my truck and stared at him for a moment. "I think I saw Chloe Beaumont."

"Wow, that's a name I haven't heard for a long time." He studied my face. "What did she say?"

"I didn't speak to her," I said.

"Why not?" he asked.

I gestured with a tilt of my head. "She was across the street. I was going to walk over there when you showed up. When I looked back she was gone. It's probably for the best though. You know, let sleeping dogs lie and all that."

He shrugged. "If you say so. What do you think she's doing back here?"

"I guess to see her uncle."

His eyebrows drew upward. "Maybe. You haven't mentioned her name for a long time. But I'm not stupid. You haven't forgotten about her," he said.

"I don't even want to talk about this," I said.

He held his hands up. "Hey, whatever. You always keep that crap in and that doesn't help anything."

"I've been doing fine for this long, I think I can manage for a while longer."

"Yeah, whatever you say." He ran his hands through his hair.

"Just don't go looking for her or do anything stupid like that," I said.

He shrugged. "It's none of my business."

"I'm going for my lunch now. You sure you don't want to come?" I asked.

"Nah, I got a few errands to run too," he said.

I'd grab my burger and get the hell out of there.

Just when I thought I was in the clear, getting out of there Porter Brennan approached. I'd never seen the man wearing anything other than short-sleeved button-down shirt and black pants. He was the local building inspector who took his job a little too seriously. All I wanted was some time to think about what had happened and now everyone in town wanted to shoot the shit.

"Well, if it ain't the Kenner boys. Grant and Ty, how the hell are you?" He smacked Ty on the back.

"What's going on?" I asked with a nod.

"Not a whole hell of a lot," he said with a cheesy smile.

Porter thought he was God around this town because he could say yes or no to any new building plans. He'd stopped a lot of new places around town because he wanted things to stay the same.

"Just heading for some lunch." I looked in the opposite direction, hoping he'd take the hint. I thought he knew that he wasn't one of my favorite people.

"How's your momma and daddy?" he asked.

I glanced in the direction of our parents' store. "They're good."

Ty still hadn't answered him. Ty liked him even less than I did.

"So what are you all up to today? Aren't you supposed to be out there on that bayou looking for people who aren't supposed to be fishing?" Porter chuckled.

My brother tensed at Porter's question. I was the game warden for the area. Yes, it was my job to make sure people weren't doing something they weren't supposed to. Porter was just upset that I had asked for his fishing license.

"What were you all looking at?" He cast a glance around the area.

"A woman," my brother answered.

Porter nodded. "Good-looking?"

I glared at him.

"It was good to see you all. I need to go turn down some building permits. See you later." He laughed and waved as he walked away.

"What a jackass," Ty said.

Now that Chloe had gone, I didn't want to hang around any longer. "All right, I have to go. See you later," I said as I walked toward the diner.

CHAPTER THREE

Chloe couldn't allow herself to be distracted by memories

I couldn't believe I'd seen Grant Kenner. After all these years, he still looked as handsome as ever. Actually, I had to take that back—with his strong chiseled features and muscular body, he looked better than he had when I'd left Belle Grove. I'd always loved running my fingers though his thick hair.

I wasn't sure if he'd seen me and I hoped that he hadn't. I just wanted to get out of there before he did. I should have known I wouldn't be able to sneak back into town without seeing him. My uncle had tried to talk about Grant a few times, but I'd always cut him off. If I could just get in and out in a hurry maybe I could avoid seeing Grant again.

I made my way through the winding back roads to the edge of town. It had been ten years, but I still remembered the roads as if it was yesterday. I had a lot of great memories of this place, but there were bad ones too. I had moved away so that I could create new memories. Well, at least that had been the plan. The ones that had been created since I'd left didn't seem to be as special. That was something I needed to work on when I got home. There was no reason why I shouldn't make good memories with my new life. It was time for me to start.

I made it to a paved road that was covered with tall trees. It was a secluded area. My uncle liked to live a little off the beaten path. He'd found the perfect spot this time. I pulled down the road and I hoped that I really had the right location. It was a dead-end street and the houses were spaced out with a lot of room in between. Well, what I could see of the houses. The tall trees were so dense it was hard to make sure that there were homes at the end of the driveways.

At the end of the road was a gravel driveway. The numbers were on the rusty mailbox at the end of the drive. I turned in and pulled the car down the long driveway. The small white ranch house came into view. My uncle's car wasn't parked out front. He must have taken off in his car. I was sure that he would be back soon and this trip would all be for nothing.

After pulling up and shifting my car into park, I peered around at the landscape, but didn't notice anything unusual, except for one little thing. The stack of newspapers on the front porch had started to grow. Someone had placed them into a neat pile by the door.

I turned off the ignition and climbed out from behind the wheel. What would I do first? That was of course if in fact Uncle Taylor wasn't there. Stepping through the tall grass, I moved around the back of my car and up the sidewalk toward the front porch. Uncle Taylor couldn't really maintain the lawn from wherever he'd taken off to, but surely he wouldn't be gone for much longer. My uncle liked to keep his home neat and the lawn work was one of his favorite things. I stepped up to the porch and peered down at my feet. Yes, someone had definitely taken the time to stack the newspapers. It was probably the girlfriend. My uncle had just forgotten to stop the paper.

I stepped around the newspapers and up to the door. I pulled open the screen door and knocked. As I waited, I glanced around for any other oddities. Of course Uncle Taylor wouldn't answer, but I had to try anyway. The house was surrounded by trees like a vegetated fortress. It seemed easy for someone to disappear into the trees. There were other houses around, but it still seemed as if this place was cut off from the world. If I screamed, would another living soul hear me? That was a scary thought. I was letting the setting creep me out and I needed to shake that off.

I knocked again, but no one answered, so I knew that apparently what Gina had said was correct. If he was in there he would have answered my call. She had said the police had been out to check on him and didn't suspect any foul play. I pulled out my cell phone and dialed her number. She answered on the second ring.

"I'm here at my uncle's house," I said.

"Can you wait there and I'll be right over?" she asked.

"Yeah, sure."

I wasn't sure why we needed to talk here. Wouldn't it be better if we went to someplace slightly less secluded? After hanging up the phone I wondered what to do until she arrived. Being alone at my uncle's house made me uneasy and nervous. I had to do something to keep my mind occupied.

While I waited for her to arrive, I decided to take a look in the windows. I wasn't sure what I was looking for, but I had to do something to stay busy. Maybe I'd see something that would give me a clue as to where he was. Yeah, that was highly unlikely from the window, but I'd give it a try.

I stepped off the porch and over to the windows that lined the front of the house. There were three along the front. I stepped through the mulch and bushes and up close against the house. The curtains were pulled back and I got a good view of the inside.

As far as I could tell there was nothing out of place. Everything looked neat and orderly. The sofa and chair were sitting in the room with a coffee table in front. It actually looked as if he'd cleaned. I knew I liked to leave my home clean when I went on a trip. I hadn't had time to do that before I came here. There were very few used dishes out and no unfinished business. Someone had to know where he'd gone. There had to be someone he would have told.

I couldn't handle hanging out there any longer. I had to do something constructive so I decided to walk over to the neighbors' home and ask if they'd seen my uncle. Of course I had no idea if the neighbors knew each other, but if it was anything like the Belle Grove I knew, then they would. Everyone had known everyone's business when I'd lived here and I doubted it had changed.

I stepped down the driveway and out onto the road. There was a little more light left in the day, but the trees still hung overhead, blocking out the sun.

After making it to the next driveway, I stepped forward, but paused, soaking in the view. The small ranch house looked a lot like my uncle's and it would be easy to mistake one for the other. I walked down the gravel drive and the entire house came into view. It was a light-colored brick ranch about the same size as my uncle's. I stopped in my tracks when I saw the man standing in the driveway. What was he doing here? I'd seen him twice in one day—what were the odds?

Grant Kenner and I had a history going all the way back to high school. He'd acted as if he'd loved me, but I'd soon found out that was all a lie.

I had no desire to see him again. And I definitely didn't want him to see me. There was nothing left to say between us. Sure, it had been a long time, but that was even more reason not to bring up the past. I wanted to get out of there before he noticed me. I spun around and rushed back toward the street. Why did the driveway have to be so long? I cursed the gravel crunching loudly under my feet. It was taking me forever to get out of there. It was as if an invisible force was holding me back and slowing me down. Of course that was all in my mind.

"Chloe, wait," he called out to me.

Damn. It was too late. He'd seen me. What would I do now? I could run and act as if I hadn't heard him. But he'd called my name so loudly that I was sure all of Belle Grove had heard him. That would be stupid of me if I acted that way. I had no choice but to confront my past.

I turned around to face Grant. For the first time in ten years our eyes met again. It was as if I'd never left in that split moment. My stomach flipped as if I'd just plunged off a bridge in free-fall. My body tingled all the way to my toes. I hadn't expected my body to react in such a way.

Needless to say this was an awkward situation. The words wouldn't come. He walked close to me and luckily I didn't run away this time. When he was close to me it was as if the wind had been knocked out of me.

"Hello," he said, looking me straight in the eyes.

"Do you live here?" I asked.

He nodded. "Yes, I do. How did you find me?"

I snorted. "I didn't know you lived here and it was purely by accident."

He looked me up and down.

"I wasn't looking for you," I added.

"You look great," he said with a little smile. "What are you doing here?"

I gestured over my shoulder. "I was looking for my uncle. Have you seen him?"

"I guess your uncle didn't tell you that we are neighbors?"

I shook my head. "No, he didn't share that information."

Of course I didn't tell Grant that I had always stopped my uncle any time he had wanted to talk about any of the Kenner clan.

"I haven't seen your uncle for a few days. He usually stops by to say hello. Did he go on a trip?" His face lit up with each word. Grant's handsome face was made to fill women with lust and longing.

"I'm not sure where he is. That's why I'm here." I tried to look away.

"You came all this way just to check up on him?" Grant asked.

"You could say that, yes. His girlfriend called and was concerned about him. Apparently they had an argument and he left."

"I'm sure he will be back soon." He flashed a comforting grin.

I nodded. "Well, that's what I told her too."

"She is concerned," he offered.

"My uncle didn't tell me that you were neighbors," I said.

"Well, I guess that was something he didn't think you'd want to hear," he said.

I wasn't even going to answer that. It was time for me to get out of there. No matter how good he looked in his tight shirt and well-fitting pants or what kind of memories flashed in my mind.

"Chloe?" a woman called out from behind me.

I spun around and spotted Gina DeWitt walking toward me. Thank goodness she had showed up. It was perfect timing. Now I could get out of there with the perfect excuse. How did she know where to find me?

"You found me," I said.

She nodded as she looked from me to Grant. "I thought maybe you'd disappeared too," she said with a frown.

In spite of my best attempt I couldn't take my eyes off Grant. "It was nice seeing you."

This seemed awkward and surreal. Was that the best comment I could come up with? After all this time? I had to put on my best face and not let on how I felt inside though.

He offered a gentle smile. "It was good to see you again, Chloe."

He almost sounded sincere.

CHAPTER FOUR

Grant couldn't get her out of his head

I wasn't going to lie. I'd thought about Chloe all night long as I tossed and turned in my bed. How long would she be in town? Would I see her again? Finally, I forced myself to stop. If she wanted to see me she would have let me know a long time ago. I wouldn't push myself on her.

It was the next day and I'd pulled up in front of my parents' store, Kenner's. I walked through the door and readied myself for the questions that would come from my mother. I loved her more than anything, but she wasn't bashful about asking questions. More than anything she wanted to see me with a wife.

My mother Elaine was a petite woman, but no one who knew her would ever let her size fool them. She was a tough one and she didn't put up with anything from anyone. Her once-dark hair was now sprinkled with gray. As usual she was stylishly dressed, today wearing brown pants and a white blouse.

"Do you like my new outfit?" she asked.

"Looks good." I winked.

Like I knew the first thing about women's clothing. My father Wayne had his head buried in the morning newspaper. He peeked over the top with his glasses at the tip of his nose. "It's about time you showed up."

Movement caught my attention. Ty walked from the back room of the store. Since he wore his uniform I figured he was heading to work soon. My father put the paper up and started reading again.

My mother wrapped her arm around Ty's waist. "Two of my favorite guys. Now if the rest of my boys were here it would be perfect."

I had three other brothers. The rest of them were sprinkled around town, but I didn't talk with them often because we all had strange work hours. Stephen was a firefighter and Seth was a lawyer. Miles was the doctor. We had all the professions covered, which made my mother extremely happy. She eyed me for a moment and I knew the questions were about to start. She'd probably already asked Ty questions, now it was my turn.

A little grin crossed her lips. "I heard that Chloe Beaumont is back in town. My, isn't that something. She finally came to her senses and came back to Belle Grove. If she's smart she'll stay this time."

I stared at Ty. He shrugged. So that was how he'd gotten away from her questions. Why had he told her? Yeah, it was just so he didn't have to answer her questions about his dating life. Five sons and not one of us was married or had children.

My mother felt as if she had been a failure because of this. I decided to avert the conversation. The more I was in control of the topic the better off I'd be.

I looked at Ty. "Did you know about the police checking on her uncle?"

"What's wrong with her uncle?" my mother asked.

My father looked over the top of the paper again.

Ty frowned. "What are you talking about?"

"You're a cop, I figured you'd know about this. Her uncle is missing," I said.

My mother let out a little gasp.

I leaned against the table. "Chloe seems to think he just took off."

"Why would he do that?" my mother asked.

My father set the paper down. He was fully invested in the conversation now.

"Chloe says that her uncle and his girlfriend had a disagreement and after that she said he came up missing. I guess he didn't answer the girlfriend's calls," I said.

My mother shook her head. "Well, did they check his house, for heaven's sake?"

I sat on the edge of the table. Usually my mother would have warned me against this, but she was too engrossed in my story. "The police went out for a welfare check at his place. Said they couldn't find anything suspicious."

My mother frowned. "That doesn't make any sense."

"I didn't know that they'd been out there." Ty ran his hand through his hair. "I thought I would have heard about that."

I folded my arms in front of my chest. "Yeah, I thought you would have heard about it too."

"Well, I'll look into it and see what details I can find out," he offered.

"I'm sure Chloe would appreciate that."

"So are you going to talk with her again?" Ty asked.

I studied my shoes. "There's no reason for me to talk with her. I'm sure if something is really wrong then Ty can talk with her."

"She probably needs someone to talk to right now," my mother said in a warning tone. "Tell him, Wayne. Tell him that the girl will need a friend."

"She'll need a friend to talk to," my father said in an even tone as he pulled the paper in front of his face again.

"I'm sure it's nothing. Chloe can handle it. She was always a tough girl," I said.

My mother started picking up things from the counter. That was her way of telling me she wasn't happy with my statement.

Ty grabbed his cup of coffee. "I have to go. I'll let you know what I find out," he said as he kissed my mother's cheek.

"Yeah, thanks," I said over my shoulder as he walked out the door.

"Do you really mean what you said? Do you think there's nothing wrong with her uncle?" she asked.

I stared for a moment and then nodded with a smile. "Yes, I think he's fine."

The words slipped out, but I couldn't deny that there was a slight bit of doubt in my mind. That was only normal though, so I pushed the uncertainty to the back of my mind.

I reached down and gave her a hug. "I'll see you later. I have to get to work."

"Will you do me a favor?" She used her sweetest voice.

I should have gotten out of there before I let this happen. I knew I wasn't going to like this favor. She knew I'd do anything for her, but some things she asked for were just too much.

"Will you find Chloe and make sure she is okay? And tell her to come in here and see me." She pleaded with her big brown eyes.

I didn't tell her, but if Chloe wanted to see her I was sure she would stop by without having to be told. I nodded. "I'll see what I can do." I figured that was a vague enough answer that would get me off the hook.

My father rattled the newspaper. "Yeah, see you later, son."

Luckily I made it outside without another question and hopped into my truck. My office was tucked away next to the bayou. A large covered boat dock was near the parking lot. When I pulled up I noticed someone was out there by the dock. And it wasn't just anyone… it was Chloe. My heart thumped in my chest when I saw her. What was she doing?

Chloe looked sexy in her jeans and tight pink T-shirt as I watched her from afar again. She hadn't noticed that I was around. Apparently, she'd done enough research to know that her uncle's boat was docked here. She was walking around the edge of the dock. Something told me that she had no idea what she was doing. Sure, she was from the bayou, but that didn't take away from the fact that she was clumsy and didn't know the ins and outs of the area. I remembered the time she fell trying to step off the bleachers in high school. When I'd grabbed her to break the fall she'd landed on top of me. We'd both tumbled to the ground, but having her soft body next to mine, I wasn't about to complain.

I inched a little closer, but she still hadn't looked back and noticed me. She was peering out over the water. What was she looking for? When she finally stepped to the side, she slipped on the wet ground and tumbled to her knees. I sprinted across the lot toward her. Within seconds, I was at her side with my hand on her arm helping her to her feet. She let out a gasp when I touched her.

"Sorry, I didn't mean to startle you," I said.

She scowled as she steadied herself. I knew by the look that she was surprised to see me again.

"What are you doing here?" she asked as she wiped her pants off.

Her dark hair was pulled back in a loose ponytail. Her face had a natural glow and her green eyes shone in the sunlight.

I motioned with a tilt of my head. "I work here."

She looked over my shoulder. "Your office is in there?"

I nodded.

She scowled. "When did that happen? It wasn't always here, was it? Heck, that building is new. I used to come out here to the dock all the time and never remembered seeing it."

I motioned toward the building with a tilt of my head. "It's been here about two years now. So what are you doing here?"

She averted her eyes and blew the brown lock of hair from her eyes. "I came here to check on my uncle's boat. Do you know when he was here last?"

"Just a few days ago, I think. He waved but I didn't get a chance to talk with him."

She peered out over the bayou. "When was the last time you saw him at his house?"

"Since the houses are far apart with trees, I didn't see him often. He came over a few weeks ago. You haven't heard from him?" I asked.

She crossed her arms in front of her chest. "No, I haven't. Did he say much when he came over?" Chloe stared at me with her big green eyes and I lost my concentration for a moment.

"Well, you know he was going to build a house on that land that he owned," I said.

"He had mentioned it. Do you know when he was starting that project?" she asked.

I shook my head. "He didn't say. Sorry I don't have more information for you."

I watched her for a moment. There was more that I wanted to ask, but I didn't know if it was the right time. Would there ever be a right time?

Finally, after a long silence, I said, "I told my brother that you were back in town."

A sweet smile slid across her lips. "I bet he was surprised about that."

"He was surprised. He didn't know that the police had checked on your uncle." A strand of hair fell near her cheek and I wanted to reach out and brush it away.

She tucked the hair behind her ear. "Really? I figured since it's a small town everyone would know everything."

"You know this isn't the typical small town," I said.

She nodded. "Yeah, how could I forget? So your brother didn't know anything?"

I shook my head. "No, he said he'd ask around though."

Chloe grinned. "I'd appreciate that."

We exchanged a look. Was she going to say more? It had been so long and there were a lot of questions I wanted to ask. I wouldn't overstep my boundaries though. I would wait for her to make the first move. The problem was I didn't think she would make the first move.

"You know there were a lot of newspapers piled up by his front door," she said.

"And you think that means something is wrong?" I asked.

She waved her hand. "No, I mean, I don't know what to think."

"He probably forgot to stop the paper before he left. Especially if it wasn't a planned trip. If he had an argument with his girlfriend and just took off, I doubt he would have thought of that."

"Maybe so," she said as she looked out over the water. I studied her pretty face. If she knew I was watching her she never let on. Finally, she turned to me and said, "I should go."

I'd barely had a chance to nod when she turned and walked away. I watched her as she made her way across the parking lot and to her car. She didn't look back, but I knew she felt my eyes on her. How could I not stare? Chloe climbed in her car, cranked the engine, and pulled away.

I didn't know why the universe had brought her back into my life, but I was glad that she was there.

CHAPTER FIVE

Chloe can't run from her past

As I walked along the sidewalk of my hometown I realized that I was almost smack dab in front of the store that Grant's parents owned. They'd been running that store since I could remember. Grant used to work there after school. I wished I hadn't been daydreaming. Now I had to either turn around or cross the street. I decided to cross the street because I wanted to go into a shop a couple doors from theirs. I stepped over to the curb but suddenly there was a traffic jam in Belle Grove, making me have to wait.

I made the mistake of turning around and looking back at the store window. There was a little face peering out at me. Damn. It was Grant's mother. If I turned around and acted as if I didn't know her would she go away? No, that would be incredibly rude of me. She'd never done anything to me and she'd always been nice. There was no need to be mean to her. She wasn't responsible for her son's actions. Since I still couldn't cross the street, I knew that my only option was to turn around and acknowledge her.

Just as I looked back to wave at her, she was coming out toward me. There was nowhere for me to hide. I would have no choice but talk with her. Would she be mad at me for leaving her son? After that many years I hoped that she had forgotten about what had happened. It was her son's fault and not mine so she couldn't hold me responsible.

I smiled at her as she marched toward me. When I found my uncle he was getting an earful from me for making me come back to Belle Grove.

"Chloe Beaumont, is that you? Oh, my goodness. It's so nice to see you." She spread her arms out, moving in for a hug.

I offered a wide smile. "Hello, Mrs. Kenner. How are you?" I wrapped my arms around her and squeezed back.

She stepped back and looked me up and down. "You look great."

I smiled again. "So do you. I love what you've done with your hair."

She fussed with her hair. "Oh, I am due for a trip to the beauty parlor. What are you doing standing out here? You need to come inside and say hello to Mr. Kenner." She motioned for me to follow her.

I followed her inside. The store was just as I remembered it. Some things had changed like new items and displays sitting around, but other than that everything was the same. The store carried everything from food to household supplies. Of course being back in there brought back a flood of memories. That was the case with just about everything in town though. My stomach dipped a little when I thought about saying hello to Grant's father. Maybe he wouldn't be as friendly as Grant's mother. He'd always been a jokester, but that had been a long time ago.

We passed by the small displays of snacks and candy toward the office at the back.

When I reached the back office I spotted Mr. Kenner sitting at a desk. He had the newspaper up in front of his face. I remembered he did that every morning. He pulled the paper down and a smile crossed his lips. He winked and said, "How have you been, young lady?"

"I've been fine, Mr. Kenner. How are you?"

"I can't complain. Good to have you back." He pulled the newspaper back up and began reading.

That was the extent of his small talk. Nothing had changed though. That was always his character. He didn't look different either, just a little gray hair. He was handsome like his sons.

"Can I get you anything?" Mrs. Kenner asked.

I shook my head. "No, I'm okay. I was just headed to buy a couple of shirts. I didn't pack enough clothing."

She nodded. "I'm really sorry about your uncle. I heard the news. I hope you locate him soon."

"Thank you. I'm sure he'll call soon. He probably doesn't know what kind of worry he's caused me," I said.

Her charm bracelet jingled as she waved her hand dismissively. "Men are like that sometimes. They just don't think." Mrs. Kenner cast a glance in her husband's direction, but he didn't take his gaze away from the newspaper. "I've been worried about you," she said.

"Well, thank you for thinking of me. How have you been?"

She smiled and waved her hand through the air. "Working in this place. Someday we're going to retire."

I picked up a package of gum and then placed it back on the display case. "That would be nice. The place hasn't changed much." I looked around again. Mr. Kenner turned the page of the paper, but didn't look up.

"Not much different as far as food to sell. That's just the way I like it though. I don't like change." Mrs. Kenner stared at me and I averted my gaze.

Was that comment meant for me too? As in I shouldn't have changed by leaving town?

"Are you staying in Belle Grove?" she asked.

I couldn't avoid her stare any longer and I wouldn't be able to avoid the question. I shook my head. "No, I'll be going back to Arizona as soon as I find my uncle."

She frowned and shook her head. "Well, I hope you like it there. Do you have a special someone back there?"

Mr. Kenner coughed. That did nothing to stop her penetrating stare though.

"No, I don't have a special someone. I was thinking of getting a dog though," I said with a smile.

She wasn't happy with my answer. "I'm sorry things didn't work out between you and Grant."

Mr. Kenner coughed again. She'd caught me off guard with her comment. I had hoped that she wouldn't mention the past. It was too late for that now.

"Sometimes things just don't work out," I said.

"That's true." She tapped her fingers against the desk. "Perhaps this will be a fresh start though. Things change in ten years." She smiled widely and wiggled her eyebrows.

It was time for me to get out of there. There was no way to come back to the past. I glanced over my shoulder, looking for a way to escape.

"Leave her alone," Mr. Kenner said from behind his newspaper. Thank goodness someone was there to try to save me.

She waved off his comment. "Oh, I'm just having a little conversation. Nothing wrong with that, right?"

She stared at me, waiting for me to give the correct answer. I had no choice but to nod in agreement. What could I say, no?

"Now where were we? Oh yes, talking about new chances and starting over."

I looked at my phone. "Oh, look at the time. I really should be going."

Mrs. Kenner frowned and I knew she wasn't happy with my comment.

She stepped closer to me and lowered her voice. "I hope you don't mind that I ask what happened between you? You were such a cute couple."

Mr. Kenner lowered his paper. "Will you leave the girl alone? She already said she has to go. Now stop asking her questions that she obviously doesn't want to answer."

She frowned at him and I knew if he wasn't careful he'd be sleeping on the sofa tonight. Nothing was going to stop her line of questioning. I would just have to start making my way toward the door.

I stepped backward a little. "You know, it's been so long ago. I'd rather not talk about it."

"See, I told you," Mr. Kenner said.

She glared at him and then frowned at me. "Well, that's your choice, dear. I do hope that you will at least be friends now. There's no sense in fighting your feelings."

She didn't take her eyes off me. What did she know about my feelings? How did she know how I felt about her son? Any feelings I had right now would fade as soon as I left Belle Grove. It was for the best.

She stacked a few items on the desk and didn't look at me. I knew she was upset but she would get over it. I moved a few steps closer toward the door.

"Well, I hope you will come to dinner sometime." She finally looked up and noticed that I'd moved even closer to my escape.

"I sure will," I said with a smile.

I knew that I wouldn't, not after the way she'd questioned me today. And I knew she would invite Grant too.

"Great. So I will see you tonight for dinner?" she asked.

What? How had that happened? "I should go," I said, motioning over my shoulder and taking a few more steps.

I bumped into a display and it fell to the ground with a crash. Oh great. Now I would never get out of here.

I hurried and began picking up the items. "I'm so sorry."

"Don't worry about that," she said as she helped pick up the candy. "So what do you say about dinner tonight?"

I placed the last of the candy bars back on the display shelf. She wasn't going to let this one go and I didn't think there was any way out of it. If answering yes meant that I could get out of there right now I would agree. I could always call and cancel, right? I walked toward the door and she followed me. When I reached the entrance I knew that I had delayed long enough.

I released a deep breath and finally said, "Okay, I'll see you for dinner tonight."

A huge smile spread across her face. I'd had no idea it would make her this happy. Now I felt guilty about thinking I could just cancel on her. That would make her so unhappy and I didn't want to be responsible for that.

"I'm so glad you are coming. How about seven? You still remember how to get to the house, right?"

I'd never seen her so excited. "Yes, I still remember how to get there."

I wanted to ask if Grant would be there, but I already knew the answer. She was trying to play matchmaker and she wasn't being very subtle about it. How bad would dinner be though? I could try to steer the conversation to more general topics. It wouldn't be so terrible. I'd been through worse things. Not much worse, but worse.

"I'll see you at seven." I waved over my shoulder.

She clapped her hands together. "All right. I'll see you at seven."

I stepped out of the door as if I'd just been in a hurricane. What the heck had just happened to me? How had I let that happen? I obviously was no match for Hurricane Elaine. When she wanted something she was definitely going to get it. I had put up a very weak fight though. Not that it would have mattered. That whole exchange with his mother had been extremely awkward. What would Grant say when he saw me at his parents' house? He'd probably think it was my idea. Well, I'd tell him a thing or two about that. I would make it very clear that it wasn't my idea.

I couldn't wait to see the look on his face though. I guessed it was kind of sweet of his mother to want to get us together, but it just wouldn't work. I supposed that was a mother's job.

I headed in the direction of the clothing store, where I'd been going in the first place. Now I needed to find something to wear to dinner.

What was Grant's favorite color? Oh, yeah—green.

CHAPTER SIX

Grant's coming to dinner

I wasn't sure why my mother had invited me for dinner tonight. She never prepared anything for us on week nights. I hoped it wasn't bad news. My brothers hadn't been invited, which I found even more peculiar. All she had said was that she had a surprise for me.

It wasn't my birthday, so it couldn't be that. What else was there? The teasing tone of her voice had suggested that she had something up her sleeve. I hoped it wasn't another one of her attempts at setting me up with a blind date. Last time it hadn't worked out so well and she'd promised never to do it again.

My parents lived in a two-story brick house with a small tract of land. I pulled up to the driveway, but wasn't expecting to meet a car pulling out. It wasn't just any car either. I knew right away that it was Chloe. Then I saw her sweet face behind the wheel of the car. Our eyes met and she looked slightly panicked. She pulled out on the road and avoided looking over at me. What was she doing at my parents'? Now I knew what my mother's surprise had been. How had she tricked Chloe into coming over?

I was sure once Chloe had found out I would be there she had decided to leave. I wheeled my truck into the driveway and backed out onto the road again. Punching the gas, I caught up to Chloe. She looked in her rear-view mirror, so I knew she was aware that I was behind her. I wasn't holding out hope that she would stop to talk with me though. With that thought she actually sped up and I had to push the gas again. I was hoping she wouldn't crash her car just trying to get away from me.

Maybe I needed to ease up so that she wouldn't feel the need to speed. Just then my phone rang. I reached over and retrieved it from the seat. The caller ID flashed my mother's number. She had some explaining to do, but right now I didn't want to chance answering her call. I'd return her call later though and see what she had to say about this stunt.

At least Chloe wasn't speeding any more. She'd actually decided to follow the speed limit and slow down. We were quickly approaching the more populated area of town and speeding wouldn't have been a wise choice.

I flashed my headlights at Chloe, but not surprisingly she didn't stop. She was probably cussing me for following her. Even so she could at least stop and talk to me for a second. She could tell me what scheme my mother had used to get her to her house. I was stubborn and Chloe knew that. But if she didn't stop soon then I would stop following her. I didn't want to cause her any more stress than she already had.

The lights of town came into view as we approached. She would have to slow down more now that we had reached the congested area.

I didn't expect her to speed up again, but she did. She made a right turn onto Sycamore and I followed. But when I got onto the street I didn't see her car. I couldn't believe that she had actually lost me. I had to give her credit for the awesome driving skills. She had outsmarted me. That was what I got for following her in the first place. I should have taken the hint and left her alone.

When I made it to the next light I looked to my left and my right. That was when I spotted her again.

So she hadn't gotten too far away. I tapped my fingers against the steering wheel and impatiently waited for the light to turn green. When it finally switched colors, I turned left and attempted to catch up with her. It didn't take long until I was behind her again. She made the next left and I figured she was headed back to her hotel room. She was probably beyond pissed with me for following her like we were in some kind of police chase. If she'd just talk to me, then I could try to explain.

Sure enough, within a short time, she was pulling into the hotel parking lot. I pulled in right behind her. She whipped her car up to the hotel room and I wheeled into the nearest parking space I could find. I was preparing myself for the tongue-lashing she was about to give me. Chloe looked sexy when she was angry. Something told me she wouldn't want to hear that though. She probably wouldn't offer a smile either. I'd take any expression other than a sneer as a good sign.

When she opened her car door I shoved my truck into park. I jumped out of the truck and ran after her. "Chloe, wait. What is your hurry?"

When she reached her room door she whipped around and glared at me. "Why in the hell are you following me?"

Wow. I hadn't expected to get that much of an evil glare. She looked like she wanted to punch me in the stomach. I had really pissed her off this time. Like she wasn't already mad enough with me. This hadn't helped.

"I want to talk with you."

She placed her hands on her hips. "Well, you've got me now. What do you want?"

"Why didn't you stop?" I asked.

"Because I didn't want to? Why would I stop in the middle of the road to talk with you?"

She did have a point there. "You could have pulled over somewhere so we could talk," I said.

"We're talking now, but all you're saying is why I didn't stop."

"I was just surprised to see you pulling out of my parents' driveway. I guess my mother got to you somehow. I really shouldn't be surprised. She's sneaky like that."

A slight smile crossed Chloe's lips. "She is sneaky. She's very good at it. Why were you really following me?"

"I told you I want to talk."

"Do you know that was trying to get away from you?"

"I sensed that by the speed race you had going on back there," I said with a smile.

She bit her lip. "I was just trying to get out of there."

"Before I got there, right?"

Her right eyebrow shot up. "You got it."

"Why did you go in the first place? You had to know that she was trying to set you up."

"She invited me for dinner. How could I say no?"

"She does have a way of making you feel guilty."

"Yes, she does have a talent for it. Anyway, I thought it wouldn't be such a bad idea. But then I decided it was a bad idea after all."

"What made you decide that?" I asked.

Chloe looked down at her feet. Apparently she wasn't going to answer me. But I knew what made her come to that decision without her answering. She didn't want to face me. I had forced her to do that now. I had to admit that the dinner probably would have been awkward with my mother trying to play matchmaker all evening.

"Why did you decide to go?" I thought I'd try again to get that answer from her.

She shook her head. "You know why, so stop trying to get me to tell you."

I shoved my hands in my pockets. "Sorry. Don't blame my mom, okay? She was just trying to be nice. I know she didn't mean any harm."

Chloe nodded. "Of course not. I know she just wants the best for you."

Yeah, and the best for me as far as my mother was concerned was Chloe. I couldn't say that I disagreed with her either.

Chloe stared down at her feet again and then finally said, "I should go now." She met my stare.

I nodded. "Yeah, I'm sorry about following you."

At least she'd talked to me for a few minutes. After another few seconds she smiled and then turned to open her door. I watched as she stepped inside. She turned and looked back at me. I smiled and she gave a little grin then closed the door. I stared at the closed door for a moment longer before finally turning around and climbing back into my truck.

I released a deep breath and cranked the engine. I couldn't believe my mother had invited her. I thought my mother knew that we weren't really on friendly terms. Hell, I wasn't sure where we were. Our connection was awkward to say the least. I had to give my mother credit for trying though. I wouldn't put it past her to try again either. Chloe would have to keep her distance if she didn't want to fall victim to my mother again. But she'd probably already figured that out.

As I got ready to pull my truck out of the parking lot, I spotted a car leaving. It had turned its lights on and pulled out from a parking space nearby. I hadn't even noticed that anyone was sitting in the car. When had they gotten in? When I looked closer, I thought I recognized Porter. It wouldn't be a surprise to see him at the hotel if what I'd heard about him was correct. He liked to meet the ladies where their husbands wouldn't see them. But still I didn't trust that he hadn't been watching Chloe. The creep had some explaining to do. What the hell was his problem?

When he pulled out I turned right onto the street and followed his car. He wasn't driving fast like Chloe and he didn't seem to care if I followed him or not. I'd like to ask him a few questions, but I doubted he'd give me a straight answer anyway. I wouldn't follow him for long, but I was curious where he was headed. Plus, I wanted to make sure that he didn't go back to the hotel tonight. He needed to stay away from Chloe and I was going to make sure he knew that.

A red light caught me as he drove on through. There was no way I would catch up with him. When the light finally turned, I took off, but I didn't see his car anywhere. I thought about turning back and checking the hotel one last time, but if Chloe caught me driving by again she would surely never speak to me again. Besides, he was probably going home now that he knew that I had followed him out of the place. I hoped that Chloe had locked her door. I'd drive by in the morning and check on her—well, not actually go up to the door, but just make sure her car was there and the inspector's car wasn't. But right now I decided to go home. It had been a long day and I needed to crash.

The night was dark and only the headlights of my truck sliced through the black as I headed home. I drove down my street, but didn't turn into the driveway. Instead I drove on past and pulled into her uncle's place. I wasn't surprised to see that there weren't any lights on and his car wasn't in the driveway. It didn't hurt to check though.

When I walked in my door I threw my keys on the table and went straight for the fridge to grab a beer. I plopped down on the soda and flicked on the TV. When my phone rang again I grabbed it and checked the caller ID. It was my mother again. This time I was going to make her explain her little plan. The plan that had backfired on her. Plus I needed to persuade her never to try anything like that again. Who was I kidding? That would never happen. She was about as stubborn as Chloe. I'd never realized how much they had in common.

CHAPTER SEVEN

Chloe's determined

The diner was at the end of Main and Elm. It was one of those places that served everything with a good helping of grease. I usually made a feeble attempt to absorb some of it with my napkin, but who was I kidding—smashing a napkin on my food would make little difference to the healthiness of the cuisine. Gina had picked the place to eat though, so I would make the most of it.

She whipped the car into the parking space and cut the engine. "I don't have much of an appetite lately," she said as she unfastened her seatbelt.

I opened the car door. "You need your strength, so just try to eat what you can."

We walked through the door and the smell of bacon and coffee smacked me in the face. The place had been remodeled since I'd been there. Apparently there was a new owner. Windows lined three walls, letting in light from almost every angle. Booths were along the walls and tables were in the middle of the space. It was a typical retro-style diner.

Gina pointed at a booth across the way. "How about there?"

"That's fine," I said, looking around at the gawking faces.

Surprisingly, I recognized a couple people. Well, I guessed I shouldn't be too surprised. Most people never left Belle Grove.

The waitress didn't speak as she dumped the menus on the table. Maybe it was just me, but she seemed a bit hostile.

"Does she not like us?" I asked.

Gina picked up a menu. "She used to date your uncle."

Oh… I looked over at the woman as she stood behind the counter. She wore the diner's uniform of a blue shirt and black pants. Her blonde hair was pulled back in a tight ponytail.

"I take it she knows that you are seeing my uncle," I said.

Gina nodded, but didn't look up from her menu. "Yes, she knows. I don't know why she cares, she broke up with him anyway."

I stared at the woman for a moment until she looked over and caught me. I grabbed the menu and buried my face in it. This situation was too awkward.

The sensation that someone was standing next to the table grabbed my attention. As much as I didn't want to I know who was there I had to look over. I peeked over the top of the menu, expecting to see the waitress. A man was staring at us from the next booth over. A couple of men sat across from him with their backs facing me.

Gina looked over just then and frowned.

"Who is he?" I asked.

"That's Porter Brennan, the building inspector that Taylor had words with the other day. He's the reason for our fight."

The man watched me for a moment longer and then said, "How are you, ladies? Are you new in town?"

I stared at him. "No, Belle Grove is my hometown." What business was it of his?

"It must be nice to be home." He flashed a fake smile.

I nodded. "Yes, it is." Trying to avoid more conversation, I studied my menu.

"That's really nice, real nice," he said.

I glanced at Gina and she frowned. What exactly did this man want?

"So, you're a long way from your new home. I bet you can't wait to get back." He still scrutinized my every move.

When I looked at Gina, she shrugged.

He continued to talk in spite of the fact that I wasn't engaging in the conversation. "Yes, I bet you're ready to get out of Belle Grove."

That was strange. If I didn't know better I would have thought he was trying to tell me something. Like that it was time for me to leave.

"Well, enjoy your breakfast, ladies. My eggs are getting cold." He nodded and flashed a fake smile.

When he stopped watching me, I asked Gina, "That was strange. Do you know him?"

She nodded. "Not very well. I know he is the one who approves all new buildings in Belle Grove."

"Even new houses?" I asked.

She took a sip of her water, then said, "Yes, I'm sure he handles that as well."

"I imagine that my uncle had to get permission from him to build the new house." I wondered how that had gone.

The waitress made her way back over to our table. "Gina, how are you?" She didn't seem too sincere when she asked.

"I'm okay," Gina mumbled.

No other words were exchanged as we placed our orders. I decided on toast and eggs while Gina had the French toast.

"I guess she isn't happy with you. Should we be worried about our food?" I asked.

Gina shook her head. "I think she's harmless."

Well, just to be safe I was going to look for anything in my food that I didn't think was supposed to be there. Better safe than sorry.

The waitress brought the food back and not so gently placed it on the table in front of us. "Anything else?" she asked hastily.

I wasn't about to ask for ketchup. "No, thanks," I mumbled.

After she'd gone, I poured a mountain of ketchup over the top of my eggs. "So she was dating my uncle and then they broke up?"

Gina leaned in closer. "She doesn't date anyone exclusively, if you know what I mean."

I nodded. "Yeah, I think I know what you mean. Why is she so upset then if she didn't even want him?"

Gina took a bite. "I don't know," she said with a mouthful of food. People could be so strange.

When I felt eyes on us again I glanced over my shoulder. The inspector was staring again. Actually, the entire table of men was staring this time. What had we done? Was this some special diner that we weren't supposed to be in?

"Why are they staring at us?" I whispered.

Gina shrugged, but didn't look up. "I don't know."

How did she even know who I was talking about if she didn't look at them? Did this guy have something against me? Or was it my uncle? Maybe it was Gina and she didn't want to tell me.

I should have walked up and asked him what his problem was, but I didn't want to cause problems after I'd just come back to town. It was as if Gina was avoiding looking over at him on purpose. Was she afraid of him? He did seem as if he was a big bully. I just needed to get in touch with my uncle and get out of Belle Grove. There was nothing here for me now. Although there didn't seem to be much for me back in Arizona either. In a way I was lost and still hadn't found myself.

"I'll be back in a minute," Gina said, jumping up from the table.

I watched as she hurried across the restaurant toward the ladies' room. She had barely disappeared behind the door when the waitress appeared by the table.

"How's Taylor?" she asked.

So now she was going to make small talk with me?

"To be honest, Anna Louise"—I looked at her name tag—"I haven't talked with him. As a matter of fact, we can't find him."

She pulled off my ticket and placed it on the table. "Is that right?" Anna Louise didn't act surprised.

"Yes, that's right. Have you seen him?"

"I haven't seen him. He likes to go on little trips. He did that all the time. He probably just wants to get away from Gina. She tries to act sweet and innocent, but she's far from it. I wouldn't trust a word she said." Anna Louise cast a glance over her shoulder.

Okay, now I didn't know who to believe. They were both saying the same thing about the other. I didn't want to be in the middle of a love triangle.

"Will you let me know if you find out anything about where he could be or if he calls you?" I asked, handing her my business card.

"I've read some of your books," she said with a little smile.

Just then I noticed Gina coming back to the table. She frowned, but continued across the room. Anna Louise must have noticed that I was watching over my shoulder because she abruptly turned and walked away without saying another word. I felt bad because maybe she was a sweet person and I had just listened to what Gina said without knowing the facts. Anna Louise could be right, Gina could be the one who hadn't been very nice. I was already falling into their tug of war.

"Is there something wrong?" Gina asked as she made it back to the table.

I shook my head. "No, she was just giving me our tickets. She said she'd read some of my books."

Gina rolled her eyes. "Oh, she's probably just saying that. I doubt she has read anything."

Wow, Gina really didn't like this woman. I wondered if there was more to this story or was she just jealous because Anna Louise had been with my uncle? It was probably a little bit of the jealousy thing. I wasn't even going to ask because I knew Gina wouldn't be truthful.

Gina focused her big brown eyes on me. "Are you sure there isn't something else?"

"No, there was nothing else. We should go," I said as I pushed up from the table.

My uneasiness increased by the minute. The inspector was still watching us with what I could only describe as a look of disdain on his face. That was all I needed to know that it was time for me to get out of there. We walked over to the counter to pay for the food. After getting my change I turned and headed out the door. The inspector wasn't at the table anymore. I had no idea where he'd gone.

When we stepped out into the parking lot, Porter Brennan was leaning against Gina's car.

"What is he doing?" I asked. A bit of uneasiness sounded in my voice. I didn't want any trouble with this man. I didn't even know him.

"I don't know," Gina said in a low voice.

I would just tell him that I would be leaving Belle Grove soon. But what did he care if I was here anyway? The last I checked he didn't own the town. I still knew plenty of people in town and I was sure they didn't have a problem with me being here.

"How was breakfast, ladies?" he asked with a smirk as I approached the car.

"It was fine, thank you." My accent was quickly returning. Heck, it probably had never gone away. You could take the girl out of Louisiana, but not the Louisiana out of the girl.

"Good, good, I'm glad you enjoyed it," he said as he leaned against the car door. He was blocking me from getting into the car.

"You're in my way," I said.

He glared at me. "I think it's probably best if you just left Belle Grove."

"Excuse me?" I snapped.

He stood a little straighter. "You heard me."

"What business is that of yours?" I demanded.

His face turned red and he stepped closer to me. "I don't like you, that's why."

He was a lot taller and a lot bigger than me and I didn't like that he was standing so close. "You don't know me," I said.

"It doesn't matter if I know you or not," he said.

When he reached out to grab my arm, someone yelled from behind me. His expression changed and he dropped his arm. He stepped back, but he was still standing in front of the car door.

"Is there a problem here?" Grant asked as he approached.

The man stared at him for a moment and then finally said, "I have no problem."

"Is he bothering you?" Grant took a defensive stance in front of Porter.

I really didn't want any problems, so I said, "No, everything is just fine. He was just moving out of my way so I could get in the car, right?"

The man nodded as he glared at us one last time. He turned and walked away. I hoped that I never saw him again while I was in Belle Grove. I'd grown up here, it wasn't as if I was truly a stranger.

Grant turned to face me. "Are you all really okay?"

I nodded and Gina climbed behind the wheel.

"What was that all about?" he asked.

I shook my head. "I honestly don't know."

Grant frowned. "He looked as if he was about to grab you."

I nodded. "I think he was. Something tells me he doesn't like me very much."

Grant crossed his arms in front of his chest. "Does he know you?"

"I've never seen him before until I got here." I glanced in at Gina. "Thanks for coming over. I'd better go. She's waiting for me."

Grant stared for a moment and then nodded. "Take care, okay?"

CHAPTER EIGHT

Grant will always be there for Chloe

I'd never really liked Porter Brennan anyway. Why had he treated Chloe that way? He didn't even know her. Porter had come to town after Chloe had left. Not to mention he had acted as if he owned Belle Grove from the moment he'd set foot in town.

He'd moved here to take the building inspector position. From what I'd heard, Porter had lived in St. Louis previously, but that was all I knew about him. That wouldn't stop me from finding out more. I wouldn't let him treat Chloe that way. There was nothing she could have done to deserve the harassment.

I'd look into why he had acted that way. Ty would want to know why I was interested if I asked him. He'd never let me hear the end of it if he knew my probing was because of Chloe. But who else could I ask? I wanted to keep my questioning quiet because word spread quickly in Belle Grove. From what I'd heard Porter was a bit of a ladies' man around town. How he managed to attract any woman was beyond me. Had he hit on Chloe and she'd turned him down? That was a possibility.

After watching Chloe drive away, I was more than a little curious about her uncle. It was strange that he'd taken off without a word to anyone. Taylor had always been an odd one though. He'd probably just wanted to get away for a few days.

It wouldn't hurt if I went to his house and took a look around. Maybe he'd left a clue as to where he was heading. I knew that was a long shot, but I was curious now and wanted to take a look for myself. If Chloe caught me at Taylor's house she would want to know why I was there though. I didn't want to make her more nervous.

Within a few minutes I'd passed my driveway and arrived at her uncle's place. I'd almost expected to see her car in the driveway when I pulled up, but she wasn't there. I was a little disappointed, but also relieved at the same time. At least I wouldn't have to explain why I was there.

I jumped out from my truck and scanned the area. Nothing seemed out of the ordinary. If I could just find something that would give me a clue where Taylor was, then Chloe could stop worrying, although that would mean she would probably go home to Arizona.

A sidewalk lined the front of the house. Grass and weeds were beginning to get out of hand. I walked along the path toward the front door and then up the porch steps. Someone had left the stacked-up newspapers by the door. I reached down and picked up the bottom one. It was dated from a week ago. So he'd been gone a week. I'd say it was about time that he came home.

I knocked on the door, but after a minute, I realized that in fact he wasn't home just as Chloe had said. What if he hadn't left on his own? Maybe someone needed to check the house. God forbid her uncle was in the house.

After trying the door and finding that it was locked, and then trying a couple windows, I figured there was no way I was getting in that house. My only option was to call Ty. The other officers' assumption that Taylor Beaumont had gone away on his own didn't ring true for me. I liked her uncle and I didn't want to see anything bad happen to him. Not to mention I didn't want Chloe to have to deal with that. She might not want anything to do with me, but

I wouldn't let that stop me from helping her. Maybe it would be best if she didn't know that I was helping.

As I made it halfway back to my truck, I dialed Ty's number.

"What's up?" my brother asked as I answered. "I was just going to call you. Where are you?"

"I'm at Taylor Beaumont's house," I offered.

"What are you doing there?" Shock sounded in his tone.

I knew what he was thinking. "I came by to check on him."

"What did you find out?" he asked.

"Nothing much actually. There's a stack of newspapers on the porch. The first newspaper was dated from seven days ago, so I know he's been gone that long." I opened the truck door.

"Good detective work," he quipped.

"Someone has to do it," I said.

After a pause he said, "The uncle was turned down for a permit for his new house."

I jumped behind the wheel of my truck. "It's funny you mention that because I have some questions about the inspector."

"Like what? Other than he's a jerk?" Ty asked.

"I caught him giving Chloe a hard time today at the diner."

"Is that right? What were you doing with Chloe?"

I knew Ty wouldn't wait long before asking.

"I wasn't with her. I just happened to be there and saw it," I said.

"Then how do you know he was giving her a hard time?"

"I could tell by her expression."

"What else happened?" Ty asked.

"He moved toward her as if he was going to attack her. That's when I stepped in."

"Maybe I should go pay him a visit," Ty said.

"Yeah, well, I'd like to go on that visit with you," I said.

"I have to work now, but we'll track him down. I'll give you a call."

"Sounds good."

"What did Chloe say?" he asked.

"She didn't say much of anything."

"Did she talk to you?"

"We haven't spoken other than general conversation," I said.

"Maybe you should change that."

I leaned my head back against the truck's headrest. "There are probably a lot of things I should do, but I don't," I said.

"Yeah, okay. I'll call you later."

After hanging up the phone, I sat there for a moment thinking about what had happened. Chloe had looked as beautiful as usual this morning. I couldn't get her smiling face out of my mind. After all these years, she was just as I'd imagined she'd be. I had seen her picture online when I'd looked her up, but she looked even better in person.

I needed to get my mind back to the task at hand. It was time for me to get to work. Looking for her uncle would have to wait for now.

There had to be more to the fight with her uncle and Gina. I tried to think of someone who knew Gina. That was when I remembered a colleague from the next town over. He'd talked to her a few times. I hadn't known until recently that they'd had a romantic involvement, only that they'd definitely had some kind of friendship. When I got to the office, I'd look up his number and give him a call.

I cranked the engine and made my way out of the driveway and over to my office. I was so engrossed in thought that afterward I barely remembered the ride there.

I pulled into the parking lot and cut the engine. Looking out across the area, I remembered why I loved working on the bayou. The water gave me peace and the surroundings calmed me. I glanced down at the dock. Her uncle's boat was still out there in the water, just where he'd left it. Once inside, I found the number for Larry Wells, the guy who had dated Gina, and gave him a call.

"How's it going?" Larry asked.

I didn't want to waste time with small talk, so after a quick couple of questions, I segued into asking about Gina.

"Yeah, I know her, but we haven't talked much lately."

"Why do you think that is?" I asked.

"I assume it's because of her new love interest. I guess she's been too busy with him."

"Well, you know he's taken a little vacation, don't you?" I asked.

"Oh, yeah? Where did he go?" Larry asked.

"No one knows. Apparently he had a disagreement with Gina and hasn't been seen since."

"Interesting, so I guess that's why you want to know about her."

"Yes, what can you tell me?" I asked.

"She was involved with someone who came to Belle Grove recently."

"Who is that?"

"I don't know the guy's name, but I can try to find out for you," he offered.

"Is he still around?" I asked.

He paused, and then said, "That I'm not sure about."

"Do you know why he came back?" I asked.

"I guess to see if they could get back together."

"Sounds like they had a serious relationship at some point."

"I suppose," he said.

"What about Porter Brennan? What do you know about him?"

"I'll be honest, they saw each other a few times. I think it wasn't a serious fling."

"From what I hear he never has a serious fling," I said.

"Yeah, he's a real ladies' man."

"That's what I heard." Everyone in the area apparently knew this about Porter.

"I'll see what I can find out," he said.

"Thanks for the info. I'll talk to you later."

That conversation had raised more questions than answers. That was the way it usually worked though.

What would I do in the meantime? Right now I had work to do, but after that, while I waited on more information, what would I do? I couldn't let Chloe handle this on her own. Helping find Taylor Beaumont was the one thing I could do for her. Maybe it would make up for the past. Even if she didn't know that I was doing it, at least I would know that she'd had help.

I had a hard time focusing on work all day because I just wanted to get on with helping Chloe. I'd thought about it all day and tried to figure out what to do for her.

I'd had a few ideas of how to get to the bottom of this. One of them involved talking with Gina. She had to have more details on what was said right before Taylor left. If she truly didn't feel he'd left on his own, then I had to find out what she thought had happened to him. If she was close to him then she had to have at least a little bit of a clue. Who had he talked to in the days leading up to his disappearance? Had anything unusual happened? Maybe he'd had a disagreement with someone else.

After work, I climbed into my truck and headed for Gina's address. I wasn't sure if she would talk to me, but it was worth a shot. If she really wanted to find him, then she'd be willing to talk with anyone who wanted to help her. I know if I was in that situation it would be exactly what I would do. But everyone was different, and I had no way of knowing exactly how she would react. I was about to find out though. I hoped that this visit went well and that she actually talked with me.

I pulled up in front of Gina's little white cottage. A car was in the driveway and I assumed that it was hers. I wasn't sure if she would remember me. I had met Gina on a couple of occasions when she was with Taylor.

I should have waited for Ty, but there was no time to waste. I couldn't stop myself from wanting to help Chloe. Maybe if I helped her, she would actually talk to me. Hell, maybe we could go out for dinner. I'd even take going out for a cup of coffee. That would be better than nothing.

After knocking on the door, I studied my surroundings. Everything looked pretty straightforward. A large trash can and recycling bin stood by the garage. The only thing in the bin was a few newspapers. When Gina didn't answer the door, I was ready to turn around and leave. Then the lock turned on the door and opened wide. She looked shocked to see me standing at her front door. She frowned and said, "Is everything okay?" Maybe she thought I was with the police.

"Do you remember me?" I flashed a sincere smile.

"You're Grant Kenner, right?"

I nodded. "Do you mind if I ask you a few questions?"

She stared for a moment and then nodded. "Sure, what do you want to know?"

"I want to find out where Taylor Beaumont is and want to ask a few questions," I said.

She gestured for me to come inside. "Come on in."

All the blinds were pulled, making the space cave-like. Gina's appearance matched the bleak look of her house too. She had dark circles under her eyes as if she hadn't slept in days. I supposed if she thought Taylor was missing that would be enough reason not to sleep.

"What do you want to know?" she snapped.

"Can you tell me what was said the last time you spoke with him?" I asked.

She shook her head. "He was angry."

"What was he angry about?" I asked.

She picked at the edge of the pillow cushion. "Well, Porter Brennan turned down his permit. He was furious. He said he wasn't going to take that shit from Porter."

"Do you know what Taylor planned to do?" I asked.

Gina looked down at her bare feet, as if exhausted. "No, but I think he was going to confront Porter and I didn't want him to. I told him if he was going to be that stupid then I didn't want any part of it and that he should just leave."

"So that's when he left?" I asked.

She nodded. "Yes, and now I regret telling him that."

"Sometimes we say things that we regret," I said. I'd learned that the hard way.

She shrugged. "I suppose."

"Do you know if he ever talked with him?" I asked.

Gina pushed a stray lock of her brown hair behind her ear. "No, I don't know."

I crossed my arms in front of my chest. "You know, I heard something else about you."

Her expression changed and she tensed. "What's that?" she asked cautiously.

"Someone told me that there was another man here recently. He's an ex-boyfriend. Apparently he wanted to start a relationship with you again. Is that true? You know word spreads quickly in small towns," I said.

"That's not true."

I leaned against the sofa. "I think it would be best if you were honest with me. If you really want to find him you'll tell me everything."

She avoided my stare for a moment and I expected her to ask me to leave at any moment.

"Okay, it's true. I did have someone who came back here," she said.

"And what happened?" I folded my arms across my chest.

"Well, I didn't go back with him."

"Did Taylor know about this?" I asked.

She nodded. "Yes, he knew."

"Did the men speak to each other?"

"Yes, as a matter of fact Taylor asked him to leave. Very sternly asked him to leave." She waved her hands. "I don't want to talk about this."

Sometimes we had to talk about things we didn't want to, but I'd let her off the hook for the moment. "I went by his place. Don't you think someone needs to go in there?" I asked. "I don't want to upset you, but what if he's in there? Maybe he needs someone's help."

I didn't want to bring up the fact that he could be in serious danger if he was in there. Maybe he was dead. That thought had to be running through Chloe's and Gina's minds. There was only one way to find out and that was to go in his home. The other shades were drawn, so looking in the rest of the windows was out of the question.

She crossed her arms in front of her chest. "I have a key to his place."

Now she was telling me this? Why hadn't she mentioned this sooner? "Did he give you a key?" I asked.

She placed her hands on her hips. "Well, I certainly didn't steal it, if that's what you mean."

I held my hands up. "No, I didn't mean that at all. I thought maybe you'd found it after he left."

Her expression relaxed. "Oh, well, no, he gave it to me some time ago. Should I go in there?"

"Maybe you shouldn't go in there alone. I can go with you after I take care of a few things," I said.

She nodded. "Okay, just let me know."

I turned and walked toward the door. "Thanks for the information," I said, looking back at her.

Gina studied my face, then asked, "Why are you doing this?"

"I just want to help an old friend."

"I didn't know you'd been friends with him at all."

"I wasn't," I said.

I walked out the door and toward my car. Next, I had to pay a visit to Anna Louise. She had dated Taylor Beaumont too and might have details.

CHAPTER NINE

Chloe wants to know why Grant is helping her

"I spoke with Grant Kenner," Gina said when I answered my phone.

I'd been resting in my hotel room when my phone had startled me. I supposed I had been drifting off. It wasn't surprising considering I hadn't slept much in the past few days. It was hard to relax when I had so much on my mind. I sat up on the bed and positioned the phone between my cheek and my shoulder.

"Are you still there?" she asked.

"Yeah, I'm still here. You said Grant Kenner called you?"

"No, he didn't call, he came by my house," she said.

I was fully awake now. "What did he want?"

"He said he wanted to help find your uncle."

I was silent for a moment. What was he up to?

"Why was he offering to help? What did you tell him?" I asked.

"I said that would be fine. I think we can use all the help we can get. Plus his brother is the police, maybe they will take notice if he says something to them." Gina's voice was full of hope.

That was probably a long shot. I had no idea why he would offer to help. There had to be some other motive. Yes, I was being suspicious.

"He thinks we should go in the house," she said.

"Well, I suppose I would agree with him on that one, but how will we do that?"

"I have a key," she said matter-of-factly.

"What? You've had a key all this time?" My voice raised a level.

"Yes, I guess I didn't want to go into his home without his permission."

"How did you get a key?"

"If you think I stole it from him then you are wrong," she snapped.

"Hey, I didn't say anything like that," I said defensively. But now that she'd mentioned it… Maybe she was lying.

If Grant wanted to check the house then maybe he did believe that my uncle hadn't left on his own. Why would he want to help me though? Until recently, the last time I had spoken with Grant was the day I'd decided to leave Belle Grove. We'd dated, but I'd lost trust in him when I'd found out he'd been seeing someone else. Why bother staying around when he wanted something totally different than me? I had left Belle Grove without looking back and that had been the best thing I could have ever done. There was nothing for me here.

Enough with the trip down memory lane. There was no time to worry about why Grant wanted to help now.

"Well, since you have a key, we will just have to go in his house," I said.

"Grant said he would call me after he took care of a few things and then we could go."

I shook my head as if she could see me through the phone. "We don't need him to go to the house."

"Are you sure? What if your uncle is in there?"

I released a deep breath. "Then we will deal with that." I had to be strong. "We'll check the house. Maybe we can find a clue once we're inside."

"Okay, if you are sure," she said reluctantly.

I swore I couldn't understand Gina. Why hadn't she mentioned that she had a key before? I could have gone inside the house a long time ago.

I was sure Gina was a nice woman, but I hadn't figured out what my uncle saw in her. They didn't seem compatible. But he'd always dated women who were a little eccentric. Gina was no different. Other than their recent disagreement, I wondered how their relationship had been. Gina hadn't said and my uncle never got into his personal life much. What did he have to hide anyway? Honestly, I didn't care who he dated as long as she was good to him.

Even though I didn't know Gina well, she did seem genuinely concerned about my uncle. I had to assume that she was a good person.

"Okay, we'll go to his place. You want to pick me up?" I asked.

"I'll be there in about ten minutes," she said.

That would give me time to run a brush through my hair and put on some lip gloss and mascara. That was when I realized that I had no reason to wear makeup just to go to my uncle's house. Who did I have to impress? Oh, yeah—Grant Kenner.

After about fifteen minutes, a car pulled up to my door. I peeked out the window and saw Gina's white convertible. My hair would look like hell after two seconds of that top down. I grabbed my purse and headed out the door. She saw me and waved, so I hopped in the passenger seat.

"Sorry I was late. I had to stop for gas." She motioned over her shoulder.

I clutched my purse on my lap. "That's okay."

Within a few minutes, we pulled onto my uncle's street. As we passed Grant's house, I couldn't help but cast a glance. Was he home? Had he been thinking about me as much as I'd been thinking about him?

It had been hard to get him off my mind since I'd returned. I'd never dreamed it would be that tough.

We pulled into the driveway. My stomach flipped. I never thought we would find my uncle there, but what if he was in there? I shuddered at the thought. Why hadn't the police checked the house before now? Why hadn't Gina told me she had a key? That was still bugging me and I kept coming back to it. I guessed there was no point dwelling on it now.

Gina shoved the car into park and I hurried out the door. I made it to the front door before Gina did and I watched as she took her time walking up the sidewalk. The strained look on her face let me know that she didn't want to go in there.

When she reached the steps, I said, "You know, you don't have to go in. I can go in there by myself."

She pulled the key from her pocket. "Oh, no, I'm fine. I don't want you to go in there by yourself." I was glad she'd said that because I really didn't want to go in there alone. Gina handed me the key. "Here, you can open the door. After all, you are family."

"Yeah, sure." I pushed the key into the lock and turned. The door opened. I called out, "Hello?"

That was just a habit because I knew no one would answer. I stepped into the house and motioned over my shoulder for Gina to follow. She hesitated, but finally stepped into the foyer. The place looked as if he was coming back at any moment. It didn't appear as if he'd taken a vacation.

The place looked like a bachelor pad with only a plaid sofa, chair, scratched up coffee table, and TV in the living room. There was a small dining room table with four chairs sitting around. A mug and the newspaper was on the table.

I stepped over. This was the paper for the day that he'd disappeared. There was still a little stale coffee in the mug.

"We should check the bedrooms," I said.

She nodded. "His room is the one on the left and he uses the one on the right as his office."

After making my way down the hallway with Gina right behind me, I paused by the door. Finally, I grabbed the knob and turned. I didn't realize it, but I'd been holding my breath the whole time. The bed was the first thing I noticed. It wasn't made, but no one was in it either. I released a pent-up breath. I stepped into the room, but didn't see anyone. I even opened the closet door. Gina stood by the door, not stepping into the room.

I placed my hands on my hips. "Nothing seems out of place in here. Let's check his office and see what we find."

She nodded, but didn't say a word.

I eased into the room. There was a desk against the wall. The top was littered with papers. I stepped over and peered down. It looked as if they were all work papers. The computer wasn't on. I switched it on and waited for it to wake up. There was a pair of jeans tossed over the arm of the chair. I reached down and picked them up. Shoving my hand in one pocket, I fished around and then checked the other one.

"Is his wallet in there?" Gina peered over my shoulder.

I shook my head. "No, the pockets are empty."

The computer screen lit up, but it was asking for his password.

"Do you know his password?" I asked.

"No, but I have his bank info."

I looked at her with wide eyes. She must have noticed my shocked expression.

"I did some banking for him just the other day and I still have the info in my purse. I can go get it." She gestured over her shoulder.

"Yeah, that's a good idea."

I didn't think I did a very good job of hiding the sarcasm in my voice. I couldn't help it though. Gina turned around and hurried out of the room. I was sure she was thankful to get away from me and my stare. I turned off the computer and headed down the hallway to meet her.

I couldn't believe that she had his keys and bank info. That was more than a little odd, but I supposed my uncle trusted her with this information. Besides, if something strange was going on she wouldn't have shared all this information with me, right?

After a couple more seconds, Gina came back through the front door. She stuck her hand out toward me and I reached for the paper. The account info was written in what I assumed was her handwriting. This whole situation seemed so surreal. Standing in my uncle's place not knowing what the heck had happened to him.

"We could check his account and see if he used his card," Gina said as she motioned toward the paper.

I nodded. "Yeah, I suppose that's the best thing to do. I can log in from my phone. We should go back to your car though. I don't like standing here without my uncle being here."

She nodded. "I know what you mean."

We headed out the door. I peered back into the house one last time before closing the door. The place seemed sad and lonely. Almost as if it knew my uncle wasn't coming back.

Gina and I got back into her car and I immediately pulled out my phone to check his account. I was anxious as I waited for the site to pull up. Gina was leaning over in her seat trying to look over at the tiny screen.

"Do you see anything?" she asked.

"I should know in just a minute. Wait. It's asking another security question."

"What's the question?"

"It wants to know his favorite color."

"Green," she said without pause.

I guessed she knew more about my uncle than I'd thought. After punching in the word, I watched as the page loaded. Finally it worked.

I clicked on a couple links and it finally took me to the screen that I needed. The activity for his card was on the site. The charges were from the days before he had vanished. Except for one charge from today and an ATM withdrawal from two days ago.

"His card has been used recently," I said, my voice almost a whisper.

When I looked at Gina her eyes were wide. "What was it used for? Do you think the card has been stolen?"

I shrugged. "There's no way to know for sure. The charge is from a hotel in Texas."

Her body tensed. "That is odd." It looked as if my uncle had taken off on his own. "We should go to the police again," she said.

"The charges on his card aren't enough. They'll just say that it proves that he left on his own," I said.

"But that doesn't prove anything," she said.

I tapped the screen on my phone. "I know that and you know that, but they won't feel the same way."

This revelation had only added to the confusion. I would have to contact the hotel where he'd used the card.

As Gina drove along the road, she broke the silence. "Your uncle and I had talked about getting married. He wanted to build the house so we could live there together."

Gina seemed so helpless and vulnerable at that moment.

I wished there was something I could have done or said to make things better for her. All I could offer was, "I'm sorry."

CHAPTER TEN

Grant would never forget Chloe's wild spirit

I was just leaving work and had to contact Gina so that she could let me in the house. All day I had debated whether I should let Chloe know what I was doing. After all that time I still hadn't made up my mind. I wanted to share the info with her, but a part of me was afraid of what she would say. So far she hadn't told me to get lost, and that was the way I'd like to keep it. Unanswered questions were better than answered ones if the answer was something I didn't want to hear.

I made it to the parking lot when I noticed that her uncle's boat was missing. I glanced around but didn't see anyone. Other than our vehicles, there were no cars in the parking lot. Maybe her uncle had come back and taken the boat out. But where was his car?

I supposed someone could have dropped him off. I decided to go down and take a look. Maybe I'd see the boat out on the water. That scenario was highly unlikely though. I hoped that someone hadn't stolen the boat.

I made my way down the parking lot toward the dock. There were a few other boats, but they were still there. Taylor usually stopped by to say hi when he took the boat out. I'd been around the area for most of the day, so I didn't think that I'd missed him. I stepped up to the deck and glanced around. So far nothing seemed out of place or unusual. I moved down the dock and stopped at the end. I peeked to the left and didn't see anything. When I looked to the right, I saw the boat.

It wasn't far down the water, so I didn't think it had been taken out long ago. Maybe I'd just missed it by two or three minutes. The boat wasn't unmanned and it wasn't her uncle driving it either.

Chloe was on the boat. I wasn't sure what she was trying to do by standing up. Was she in trouble? Was this her distress call? I had to get to her before something terrible happened. So far she hadn't even noticed that I was watching her. Why had she taken the boat out in the first place?

"Chloe," I yelled.

She didn't look over at me. I hoped she didn't plan on ignoring me. Now was not the time to act as if I didn't exist.

"Chloe, wait there. I'm coming over," I yelled again.

She finally looked in my direction. I couldn't tell if she was happy that I was coming over or if she wanted me to stay away. The fact that she didn't flip me off was encouraging. I'd get my boat and with any luck make it over to her before she fell in. The way she was standing in that boat it was inevitable that she'd soon take a plunge.

I ran over to my boat and untied it from the dock. What had she been thinking? In all the years I'd known her, she had never taken a boat out on the water. She'd always had her nose stuck in a book. Sure, her father had taken her fishing a few times, but she'd taken a book with her then. Something must be wrong if she'd felt the need to take her uncle's boat out by herself. I hoped she'd explain exactly what she'd been thinking. She was just as stubborn now as she'd always been. Of course I'd always loved that about her.

I maneuvered the boat out onto the water and away from the dock. Once I steered in the direction of Chloe, I panicked when she was no longer there. How had she gotten away so quickly? She must have really wanted to get away from me. My anxiety increased when I thought about her being out there not knowing what she was doing. I made it a little closer to where she'd been when I noticed that she'd moved to the side and had only been out of view.

When I approached her boat she looked genuinely relieved to see me. That was something I could get used to, but I shouldn't count on it lasting for long.

"You found me," she said.

"I didn't know you were missing," I said as I got my boat as close as possible.

"I guess I'm a little lost when it comes to boats," she said with a little smile.

"What seems to be the problem?" I asked.

"I can't get the motor to stay on." Her voice was slightly panicked.

"Why don't you have a seat and I'll come over there and see if I can fix it," I offered.

She shrugged. "Okay."

"These things can be tricky."

"Are you sure?" she asked.

"Yes, I'm positive. It's my job."

She frowned and it looked as if she was a little disappointed that I'd said that. I wanted to help her more than anything, but once again I was at a loss on whether I should share that with her. I still had no idea what she was doing out there. It would be tough for her to avoid answering that question when I asked.

As she moved across the boat it wobbled back and forth. She swayed and tried to get her balance.

I reached out and grabbed her. Both boats moved back and forth and a vision of both of us falling in ran through my mind. I climbed over onto the boat. I reached out toward her and she turned around at that moment. We were face to face, her lips less than an inch from mine. I wanted nothing more than to kiss her at that moment. Her eyes met mine and for a moment I sensed that she wanted the same thing. Did I really have the nerve to kiss her? Chloe was one tough cookie and she'd likely hit me if I tried anything out of step. If I kissed her and she didn't want it, she'd probably push me off the boat.

Yeah, I didn't think it would be a wise decision to go in for a kiss. Our eyes were fixed on each other for a few moments longer, then she backed away. She swayed again, but managed to steady herself. Her face had turned a shade of scarlet and she avoided my gaze.

"I guess you're wondering what I'm doing out here," she said, still not looking at me.

"The thought had crossed my mind," I said.

I didn't take my eyes off her… I couldn't take my eyes off her.

I maneuvered myself over to the motor and gave it one pull. The engine started right away. "It acts up sometimes. Your uncle always has problems with it."

She looked a little defeated. "Thanks for helping."

There was a silence now since I didn't know what to say. The tree branches rustled in the wind and the water gently splashed against the swaying boat.

"So are you going to tell me why you're out here?" I asked.

"I thought I saw my uncle."

My eyes widened. "Seriously? Where?"

She gestured down the bayou. "I thought he was on a boat with some men."

"What were the men doing?" I asked.

"They were on a boat, of course," she said with frustration in her voice.

"Are you sure it was your uncle?"

She paused and then said, "No, I'm not sure. I only saw the back of him."

"Did you get a look at the other men?" I asked.

She shook her head. The sun shone across her pretty face and I momentarily forgot what I wanted to say. "Shouldn't we go after them?" She motioned over her shoulder.

I released a deep breath and looked down at the water. "I suppose we can look, but I can't guarantee where they went. But first we have to take your uncle's boat back."

She didn't look happy about that, but finally she nodded. "Fine, but we're wasting time."

"I'll follow your boat back to the dock. Can you get it back okay?" I asked.

She scoffed. "Of course. I know exactly what I'm doing."

I bit back a smile and climbed back to my boat. I waited until she got her boat pointed in the right direction, then I took off behind her toward the dock. She looked back a few times.

We finally made it back to the dock. I jumped off my boat and secured her uncle's boat. Chloe didn't waste any time stepping onto my boat with me.

"Okay, which way did they go?" I asked.

She pointed to our left. "That way."

"How many men were on the boat?"

"Three. Two men plus my uncle. Or what I thought was my uncle." Uncertainty filled her voice.

"Well, they have to come back sometime, so if we don't find them then I'll be on the lookout for when they return."

She nodded with a little smile.

We headed down the waterway in silence. I knew that it was unlikely we would see this boat, but I had to give it a try for Chloe and her uncle too. The boat hummed along the water and the breeze blew across the air. I glanced back at Chloe and she offered a half-hearted smile. I wished I knew what was going on in her head. Had she wanted me to kiss her? Of course she hadn't. We'd barely even spoken since she'd come back to town. Why would she want me to kiss her? But there was something about the look in her eyes.

"Do you see the boat?" she asked.

I was sorry to say that I didn't see another boat anywhere in sight.

"I don't see anything," I said.

"That doesn't mean that they're not out here though," she said with hope in her voice.

"No, it doesn't mean that, but I don't know how long it will be before they come back."

Her shoulders slumped. "I guess we can't stay out here forever, huh?"

CHAPTER ELEVEN

Chloe didn't want to fight a gator

"Do you see that?" I pointed toward the vegetation on the side of the water.

Grant followed my finger with his eyes, but didn't say anything.

"It's right over there." I motioned again.

I could have sworn I saw a set of eyes. My heart rate increased. I prayed that I hadn't seen an alligator, but I knew that the odds weren't in my favor. It was their natural habitat—there could be an alligator lurking there just waiting to make me his lunch. Now I felt trapped and helpless, stuck out there in the middle of the water.

Grant continued to stare at the area where I had pointed. His silence was making me even more nervous. If he didn't say something soon I would go crazy. What had I been thinking by coming out here? I knew all too well that there were gators in this water. Yet I still came out here anyway. I had more issues than *Vogue* magazine.

Finally, he nodded and said, "Yes, I see it now."

Thank goodness. I'd been beginning to think I was going crazy. Grant had been frozen on the spot and I'd waited for him to finally tell me what he thought it was.

I swore that was when the thing moved. My suspicions were confirmed. "Is what I think it is?" I asked with a quiver in my voice.

He nodded and casually said, "Yep."

"So? That's all you're going to say? Can't you get us out of here? That thing is going to lunge and attack us. He's watching me with his big black eyes. I think I saw him lick his lips."

Grant snorted. "You know he won't lunge at you."

"As a matter of fact, I don't know that," I said around a sigh.

"That's the Rock. He's been around here for about five or six years. Terrorizing people all over town."

I could have sworn there was laughter in Grant's voice. Did he find this funny? "How do you know it's the Rock?"

"I've seen him enough to know. I think he weighs about a thousand pounds."

"Well, it's been lovely meeting the Rock, but I think it's time that we got out of here."

Grant didn't move. "He's watching us now. Just don't make any sudden movements and he won't bother us."

"Well, I'm certainly not going over there to socialize with him," I quipped.

"It's getting dark, that's when they hunt the most," Grant said, looking up at the sky.

"Thanks for making me feel better."

"Don't worry, alligators typically don't like humans as part of their diets, although he might be tempted by your sweetness."

I scowled. "Oh, save the comedy routine."

Grant shrugged. "Of course they will eat any bad meat they can find given the opportunity."

I frowned. "Then you'd better not tempt him them."

Grant laughed. "It's mating season, so he will defend his territory vigorously."

"That sounds like a typical male," I said.

He laughed again.

"We're in his territory, so don't you think we should keep a safe distance and give him his space?"

He nodded. "We'll get out of here. Just remember to remain aware at all times. I don't know why you're surprised, you knew there were alligators in this water."

"I know, I know."

"They hide well in water, so be on the lookout for more eyes and nostrils sticking out of the water."

"Oh, please don't let there be more in the water. I think we're surrounded," I said, looking around the boat.

He glanced down. "There are no alligators around us. But just to be safe, don't dangle your arms or legs off the boat."

"You're crazy, do you know that?" I asked.

"So I've been told," he said without looking over at me.

Silence settled over us. We didn't speak and the alligator didn't make a move, although I thought I saw him blink a few times. I supposed I had been gone from the bayou for too long. I'd forgotten what it was like to live here. I had to admit I'd missed it, even if an alligator wanted me for a snack. Now I knew I missed it more than I'd realized.

"I'm glad you can remain so calm," I said.

"It's my job. Just take a few deep breaths and stay calm," he said.

"How can I stay calm?"

The alligator began to move and I must have let out a little whimper. I was being a wimp. Grant was right, I had to remain calm. Freaking out wouldn't do me any good. But my mama had known a girl who had been eaten by a gator, so I felt that my fears were somewhat warranted. The girl had been swimming in water where alligators had been known to live. I knew I would never do that.

"We just need to let him know that we are here, but no sudden moves," Grant said.

"What? No, we want him to ignore us. That way he will go away," I said.

Grant shook his head. "There's an oar right there. Make noise by slapping the water with the oar."

I reluctantly grabbed the oar and stuck it in the water. "He'll probably eat this oar as an appetizer before he jumps onto the boat."

Grant quirked a brow and then started to whistle.

"Why are you whistling?"

"Just making more noise," he said.

I started whistling *Twinkle, Twinkle Little Star*. Every little bit would help.

Just then the alligator jumped into the water. His tail whipped a slice through the water. A splash made the water ripple all the way out to our boat.

"Okay, we need to get out of here," Grant said.

Now he was saying this? I could have told him that a long time ago. As a matter of fact, I *had* told him that a long time ago, like when I'd first spotted the alligator.

He was moving closer toward us. Grant moved the boat. "Okay, we'll just go out here and give him a little more room."

"Sounds fine with me." I put the oar back in the water before he had a chance to take a bite.

Grant moved the boat farther away from the alligator. When I looked back, I noticed that we really hadn't put that much distance between us.

"It's chasing us," I said with panic in my voice.

Grant glanced back. "Damn it, Rock."

I didn't like the way he said that either. He didn't sound so confident now.

I shook my head. "I don't think the Rock is so harmless now."

"This is what I told you about. He likes to harass people and chase them."

"Oh, great. He's a jerk. Now what do we do?" I asked with wide eyes.

"We move away from him more."

We'd tried that once and it wasn't seeming to work. But I had to trust Grant on this one because what did I know about getting away from a gator? We moved along the water and picked up a little speed. That made me feel a little more comfortable. There was no way the gator could catch us now.

"Where is it?" I asked.

Grant shook his head. "I don't see it."

I released a pent-up breath. Maybe it was gone. Then again, maybe it was like one of those horror movies where you thought the killer was dead but then he popped back up. That gator might pop back up at any second.

"I think we're safe to go back over to land now."

"If you say so," I said, glancing around for those black eyes peeking out of the water.

"Remember that time old man Wilson was drunk and stomped on that gator in his back yard?"

I snorted. "Yeah, he practically fed it a baseball bat before he jumped over the fence and took off."

We'd had a view of the whole scene from Grant's window. Mr. Wilson had lived next door to Grant's parents.

CHAPTER TWELVE

Grant had forgotten just how much he had with Chloe

As much as I was enjoying being with her, we couldn't stay out there much longer. For her sake, I wished the boat would pop up, but I knew it was unlikely. The men could have gone to another dock by now.

I glanced up at the sky. Shades of purple and red streaked across the sky. Soon the sun would retire for the night, bringing darkness over the bayou. If Chloe didn't like the waters in the daylight, she would hate it at night.

"It's getting late, we should get back to the docks," I said.

I knew this wasn't what she wanted to hear by the frown on her face. The air was still sticky and hot and I wanted to grab a beer. Would Chloe want to go with me? That was highly unlikely. I knew I shouldn't even ask. Would I be able to stop myself from asking though?

She blew the hair out of her eyes. "Yeah, I guess we should go back now."

I turned the boat around and headed back toward the dock. The sun was setting quickly, so I didn't want to waste any more time. Whether to ask Chloe to go have a drink with me was stuck in my mind. What was the worst that she could say? She already barely spoke to me. It couldn't get much worse than that.

The wind gently blew her hair. If only I could run my fingers through her hair and caress her cheeks. I wondered if she felt my eyes on her. I wished I could go back and change the past. I would definitely do things differently now.

I pulled the boat up to the dock, but before I had a chance to help her Chloe had climbed off. She really was in a hurry. Did she just want to get away from me or did she have somewhere else to go?

I jumped off the boat. "Chloe, not so fast. Where are you headed now?"

She spun around and paused. For a long moment she stared at me and I waited for her to tell me it was none of my business.

Finally she said, "I have no idea what I'm doing."

CHAPTER THIRTEEN

Chloe realized Grant was too dangerous

I had to get away from him. Now was not the time for me to start having feelings for Grant, but the way he looked at me with his gorgeous eyes and smiled at me with that beautiful smile made it harder to say no. This was not why I'd come back to Belle Grove. He was the reason why I had to stay away. Surely he knew that. Heck, he was probably just being charming to mess with me. If he thought he was going to get to me then I'd show him that he was way off base.

He stared at me and I knew that I had to get out of there. Before I could turn around and run, he stepped closer.

"I was wondering if maybe… well, if maybe you'd like to go out for a drink. It's hot out and we could really use a drink to cool off." A slow smile tipped the corners of his mouth.

Oh, great. It would be hard to say no to the sexual energy that pulsed around him. A hot blush crept over my cheeks. Drinking with Grant. That would really make my judgment better. My thoughts were already impaired and there was no reason to make it worse. He was still staring at me and I knew that I'd have to give him an answer soon.

I had to say no. My desire to say yes was just old memories floating back and skewing my thoughts. Yes, that was it. I was just reminiscing about what could have been. What was done was done and it was time to move on. I didn't want to hurt his feelings any more, but this was something that I had to do. Surely he would understand that even something as simple as going out for a drink would be the wrong thing to do.

I was just about to open my mouth to say no when I noticed his gaze slowly rake over my body. A crackle of energy passed between us. Grant had aroused me as no man ever had.

Then he said, "Someone is coming out of my office."

When I turned around I spotted the person too. That was odd—it kind of looked like one of the men I'd seen on the boat. What was he doing in Grant's office? Apparently, Grant didn't know the man because he took off for the office door and around the corner. The man hadn't looked in our direction and I wondered if he knew we were watching him. It sent chills down my spine to know that this stranger could have been watching us.

Grant took off in a sprint up the hill toward his office. His strong legs powered him up the parking lot. This stranger definitely wasn't supposed to be in there.

I didn't want to be down there near the gators by myself. Besides, the other men from the boat might have been nearby watching me. I shivered at the thought. I glanced over my shoulder toward the water. The boat hadn't returned, so there was no way it could be the same man. At least I sure didn't think it could be him. Where would they have docked the boat?

Pushing my legs hard, I took off in a run uphill. Of course I wasn't as fast as Grant. My legs weren't that long and running had never been my strong point. I could do aerobics all day long, but running made me want to surrender instantly.

Grant had almost reached the office when he cut to his right a little. I figured he was going after the man. What would I do if he took off? I didn't want to be up there alone. That was just creepy. The bayou had always held a mysterious vibe; it seemed like the perfect place for scary things to lurk.

By the time I reached the office door, Grant had returned from the side of the building.

"Did you see anyone?" I asked breathlessly.

He shook his head. "No, he took off."

"Do you have any idea who it was?" I asked.

"No, I've never seen him before. Of course I didn't get a good look at him from so far away," he said.

"You know, he kind of looked like one of the men I saw on the boat," I said.

Grant scrunched his brow.

I knew it sounded crazy, but I was just being honest. "I know it couldn't have been though since the boat isn't here," I added.

He nodded and said, "I'm going to check inside."

I followed him through the door of the small building. So this was where he worked every day. It was a little cramped with a couple of desks and a few chairs scattered around. It was painted in a blah beige color and kind of dimly lit. Not a place I'd want to hang out for very long. He looked around the place and ran his hand through his hair. I started to worry about what if the person came back. Was he looking for something or someone?

"What did the person from the boat look like?" he asked.

"Well, a lot like the guy who was up here," I said. "But like you said he was far away and I didn't get a good look at him. He had dark hair and he wasn't very tall, but looked kind of muscular. He was wearing a black shirt. That's about all I know."

Grant stared at me for a moment longer and then nodded. "That's what I saw too."

"Is there anywhere else they could have docked the boat?"

He motioned with a tilt of his head. "A few miles up the bayou, I suppose."

The man could have been driven back up here, but I don't know why. That didn't make much sense, but nothing did right now. I looked around the office again.

"Did he take anything? Does anything seem out of place?" I asked.

Grant shook his head. "Not at first glance, no." He stepped over to a desk and moved a few things around. "Nothing seems out of place. My computer is still here. There's really nothing of value in here other than that. My car is still in the parking lot and so is yours."

I looked out the window into the parking lot. Both vehicles were there.

"So how did he get in?" I asked.

Grant met my gaze. "That's a question I don't have an answer to."

"Do you think it was a coworker and you just didn't recognize him?" That was highly unlikely, but maybe he'd given the key to someone.

"No, I doubt that. But I'll have to give them a call and report what happened."

The worry was evident on Grant's face and that made me even more nervous. I hated to leave him alone here, but I felt like it was time for me to get out of there. It was probably best if he didn't hang around either. The darkness had almost settled in, bringing a vast expanse of black sky.

He must have read my expression because he said, "We should leave. There's nothing to do right now."

I nodded and stepped outside with Grant right behind me. His nervousness made my stomach flip-flop. He locked the door and turned toward me.

As I walked along beside him, I said, "I'm sorry this happened."

"It's not your fault," he said with a little grin. "I'll walk you to your car. Just let me take one more peek around the building."

I nodded, but wanted to hurry up and get out of there before it was completely dark. There were too many places for someone to hide.

While I waited for Grant to walk around the building, I looked over my shoulder and out toward the water. The boat had to have docked somewhere else like Grant said. Otherwise, I was sure it would have been back by dark. But if my uncle had been on there, then surely he would have called me by now. After all, I'd left a million messages. They went straight to voicemail, which made me wonder if he'd just thrown the phone away. Or if someone had thrown it away for him. I was hoping it wasn't the later.

Grant appeared from around the building again and I released a deep breath. I'd never been happier to see him. I had been ready to run to my car. It felt as if eyes were watching me from the darkness surrounding us.

"Are you ready?" he asked.

I nodded and turned toward the parking lot. We walked across the lot in silence. I was sure he was wondering about what had just happened. At least this had stopped him from asking me out. I wasn't sure how happy I was about that though.

So he had asked me out and I had been about to tell him no. Asking him more questions sounded more and more like a good idea though. Maybe it was a good idea if we went out for that beer. We could go over what I had found out about my uncle's bank account. What harm could it do to have one beer with him? As long as it didn't turn into three or four we would be fine. I knew I could leave at any time. Okay, so if he asked again I had decided I would say yes. Maybe I was crazy for it, but I felt like it was the only thing I could do at this point.

"It's been a crazy evening, huh?" he asked with a grin.

I couldn't hold back a smile. "Yeah, I guess it's obvious that my boating skills haven't improved over the years."

He chuckled. "No, they haven't. The water never was really your thing."

I leaned against the car and wondered when he would ask me for that beer again. Maybe the moment was gone. I certainly wasn't going to ask him. A trickle of sweat ran down the side of his face. It was completely sexy. He watched me for a moment and I finally looked down at my feet. After a moment I looked up at him again. "I'm sorry if someone was messing around with your office."

He shrugged. "I'm sure it was nothing."

I nodded. "I hope so." I wasn't waiting around for him to ask any longer so I took out my keys and unlocked the car. I opened the door. "Well, thanks for coming to my rescue."

He nodded. "It's my job."

Yeah, I guessed it had been his job. It wasn't like he'd made a special trip out onto that water just for me.

"I'd better go," I said with a tilt of my head.

"About that beer..." His sentence was cut off by the ringing of a cell phone. He looked at his phone. "I need to get this."

I climbed in the car. "Yeah, I'll see you around."

CHAPTER FOURTEEN

Grant won't let a missed opportunity slip through his fingers again

As Chloe drove away I couldn't help but think about the missed opportunity. It would have been the chance we needed to talk. A chance for us to catch up and maybe a chance for me to explain what had happened in the past. If she didn't want to listen, then at least I could have said that I'd tried.

My phone was still ringing, so I looked down at the number. That was weird. I'd thought it was a call from a co-worker and sent Chloe away so that I could take the call, but now I realized that the number was different. How stupid of me.

I answered the call in spite of not recognizing the number. "This is Grant Kenner," I said.

I made my way across the parking lot toward my truck. Darkness had completely settled over the area and the stars twinkled overhead, creating a dazzling backdrop.

"This is Grant?" the soft woman's voice asked.

I unlocked the truck's door and climbed in. "Yes, this is Grant. Who is this?"

"I didn't know who else to call." Her voice was low.

I adjusted the phone to my ear. Her voice sounded as if she was in distress, but I didn't recognize her.

"Okay, if you tell me who this is maybe I can help you," I said.

There was a long silence and I wondered if she'd hung up. Finally, the woman said, "This is Gina DeWitt."

I hadn't expected a call from her. "Is something wrong, Gina?" I asked.

Her voice was barely above a whisper now. "I don't know."

"Why don't you explain exactly what is going on," I urged. "I can't help you if I don't know."

Why couldn't Gina just be honest? The events of the last few days whirled in my mind. They replayed over and over in my mind. I especially couldn't help but think about the man I'd seen by my office door and wondered if he was still hanging around. I couldn't see him if he was because I was surrounded by the darkness. How was I going to get Gina to tell me what was happening? She'd called me, so surely she trusted me, even if we didn't know each other well.

"The man approached me as I was going to my car. I had parked across the street from the bank."

"Did you know this man?" I asked.

"No, I don't know him, but he was asking about Chloe and her uncle. He wanted to know who she was and why she was in town," Gina said.

I hadn't expected her to bring Chloe's name into this. "What did he look like?"

The man she described sounded a lot like the man we'd seen at my office door. That couldn't be a coincidence.

"What did this man want with Chloe?"

"I think he wanted to ask about her uncle." She released a deep breath that sounded loudly through the phone. "What should I do?"

Whatever Chloe's uncle did shouldn't involve her.

"Where are you now?" I asked.

"I'm home now," she said.

"Are you going out again tonight?"

"No." Her voice rose.

"Okay, I'll ask around and see if I can find out who this person is," I said.

"I appreciate all your help." Apprehension colored her words.

"It's no problem. You'll call me if you run into this man again?" I asked.

"Yes, I'll call you right away."

It looked more and more as if Chloe's uncle hadn't taken off on his own.

I had to try to find this guy before he found Chloe. My heart rated increased just thinking about what this guy wanted with Chloe and what he might try if he found her. As much as I was glad she was back in town, I didn't want her to be in danger. Was she? I had no idea, but I intended on finding out. Chloe was a strong woman and I knew she could take care of herself, but everyone needed a friend in their corner and I wanted to be that friend. I hoped she'd let me.

"Are you still there?" Gina asked, dragging my attention back to the conversation.

"Yes, I'm here. Thanks for letting me know what happened, Gina. I'll find Chloe and see if she's spoken with this man yet. I'll let you know what I find out."

"Thank you for all your help," she said. "I just hope that Taylor comes back soon. More than anything I hope that nothing bad happened to him."

I sensed the worry in her voice. "I do too." I tried to comfort her with my words.

She hung up and I stared out at the darkness. Where had Chloe gone?

I couldn't decide if I should tell Chloe about the call from Gina. How would she react? No, I knew that telling her about what had happened was the best thing to do. Besides, Gina would probably tell her anyway. I hadn't thought to ask if Gina had tried to call Chloe. Maybe Gina had already warned her that someone was asking. Of course that would just make Chloe worry more about her uncle. I couldn't blame her for that because I was beginning to worry about him too. I didn't think it was like him to take off without a word for this long.

After starting the truck and shifting it into gear, I punched the gas. I had to find Chloe and make sure she was okay. I should probably look around one more time before I left, but I was in a hurry.

The truck's headlights shone across the lot and into the office. If the guy came back he'd probably wait until I was gone, although he hadn't let that stop him the first time. What would he want from my office anyway? It wasn't as if I had a connection to her uncle or to Chloe. Not anymore at least. Nothing moved in front of the lights, so I decided to get out of there.

Would it be weird if I showed up at her hotel room? Probably a little creepy to her that I knew where she was staying and which room was hers. That would freak any woman out. Of course it was a small town and something like that couldn't be kept quiet for long. That was why I was worried that the man looking for her would find her. He would find that info too.

I needed to find this man before he found Chloe. If he was really the one who had been looking around here then at least I'd gotten a look at him and would know what he looked like. I'd call Ty and see if he knew who this man might be. At the very least he could ask around for me. This was looking more and more like something the police should take seriously. Ty knew that, but apparently his hands were tied. If there was just a way I could prove that Taylor Beaumont hadn't left on his own…

It was a short drive to the hotel. But I made it in record time without speeding too much. As soon as I pulled into the parking lot I spotted her rental car. I glanced down at the paperback on the seat next to me. Chloe's latest book. Normally I wouldn't read a book titled *Love's Sacrifice*, but for Chloe I would at least attempt to read it. I wondered if she had a special someone in her life back in Arizona. Was he like the hero in her book? She wrote many characters, but the voice in my head when I read her books was always Chloe… distinctively Chloe.

I pulled my truck a few spots down from her car and shifted it into park. Turning off the engine, I released a deep breath. With any luck, Chloe wouldn't slam the door in my face.

I stepped out of the truck and over to her door. This was crazy, but I was doing it anyway. My fist froze in mid-air. Finally, I gathered up my courage and knocked on the door. I shifted from foot to foot as I waited for her to answer. No lights shone from the windows, but I knocked again, thinking maybe she'd been in the shower. Of course I had to shake that thought out of my mind.

There was still no answer. I was beginning to worry. What if the guy had been waiting for her when she'd pulled up? I wondered if anyone had seen her. I looked around the lot, but didn't notice anything unusual, just a couple of cars and the glow from room windows.

I spotted the hotel's office and decided to walk inside. Maybe if I talked to a hotel employee they could tell me if they'd seen Chloe. I stepped into the air-conditioned space. The main desk was in front with a small sitting area to the right. On the left were a couple of vending machines that hummed a little too loudly. No one was behind the desk, but as I approached a woman popped around the corner.

"May I help you?" She stared for a second and then said, "Oh, hi, Grant. How are you? How are your parents?"

I'd forgotten that Tina Baldwin had started working at the hotel. She'd worked for my parents for a short time until she found full-time work at the Belle Grove Inn. Tina had short dark hair and wore the hotel's uniform of white shirt and blue pants. The gold name tag on her shirt read manager.

"They're good. I was wondering if you'd noticed Chloe come back. Her car is parked in front of her room." I gestured over my shoulder.

"You know I can't tell you that stuff," Tina said with a smile. "What are you doing stalking my customers?"

I shook my head. "I'm not doing anything like that."

Tina chuckled. "I spotted her walking down the sidewalk as I was coming in. She said she was going over to the bar for a drink."

Had Chloe wanted to go with me to the bar? I had asked and then I'd gotten the phone call.

Tina leaned her elbows on the counter. "I guess I know where you are headed now."

I laughed. "I need to tell her something."

She winked. "I bet you do."

I waved over my shoulder. "It was good seeing you again."

"You too. Don't be a stranger," she said.

I made the short distance to the bar. When I walked inside the door I spotted Chloe right away. She was at the bar, but she wasn't alone. The inspector and another man were on each side of her. But it looked as if their company wasn't welcome.

CHAPTER FIFTEEN

Chloe almost let her lust get in the way

I'd pulled out of the parking lot in a hurry. When I glanced back in the rearview mirror, Grant was standing in the same spot, but still on his phone. I'd really dodged that one. What had I been thinking? Going for a drink with him was definitely not the right thing to do.

I was headed back into town, but I couldn't go back to the hotel. I was restless and I knew that I wouldn't be able to relax for some time. I kept replaying the day's events over and over in my mind. How could I relax with all that going on in my head?

Maybe Grant's idea of having a beer to cool off wasn't such a bad one. I'd just go by myself. There was a bar not far from my hotel. It was close enough to walk. I could park my car and walk over for a drink. It would give me a chance to clear my thoughts.

I wasn't much of a drinker and I couldn't even remember the last time that I'd been in a bar. I hoped that I didn't see any familiar faces when I got there. I didn't feel like walking down memory lane tonight.

I navigated the streets through town. The ice cream shop was still across from the high school. I'd hung out there more times than I cared to admit. Grant and I would sit and talk until the sun set and the stars popped out.

Finally we'd had to go home and I'd walk the short distance.

I still hadn't been by my old house since I'd been back in Belle Grove. The memories and pain were just too much for me to handle. I felt pulled though because I dearly wanted to see the house. I wanted to remember and I wanted to forget at the same time.

When I pulled up to the curb in front of the two-story red brick house, the memories played out as if on a movie screen. Playing with my father in the yard, helping my mother water the flowers that she'd tended to as if they were her children. Inside those walls we'd had many happy memories, but that was also where my mother had died. Hopelessness opened in my stomach, but then it hit me that my mother would have only wanted me to remember the good times. I hated the despair that I had allowed to settle in my soul. Was it too late to get rid of it? That brought me back to Grant and what had happened between us.

On more than one occasion I'd spotted Grant with my best friend Debra. The day I saw Grant and Debra hugging while sitting in his car was the day that I'd decided to leave Belle Grove. I had written Grant a letter, packed my bags, and taken off for Arizona. A friend from college lived in Phoenix at the time and had let me stay at her place until I found a place of my own. Now that I'd matured, there was some regret that I hadn't confronted Grant and Debra. There was a sliver of doubt in my mind, wondering if there had been an innocent explanation for what I'd seen. It would have been more rational of me if I'd given Grant a chance to explain. But that was in the past now and there was nothing I could do to change it. I pulled away from the curb, vowing to make some kind of change in my life.

Finally I wheeled into the hotel parking lot. I was almost sure I was the only person staying at the hotel. Unless of course there were a few couples who were just sneaking in during the middle of the day. I locked my car and headed down the sidewalk. I didn't bother going into my room before I headed out—I'd already decided that I was having one drink and then coming right back.

A breeze hit me as I walked along. It didn't last long and the humid air surrounded me again. Darkness had completely engulfed the area now.

I finally arrived at the little bar. It wasn't much more than a hole in the wall. But I knew all the locals loved the place. I walked in and the place was packed. The bar was to my left and pool tables were to my right. People were mostly by the tables, drinking, playing and talking. I had hoped that I could just head on over to the bar and blend in with the crowd. No one would even notice me or know that I was around. That was probably too much to ask. What had I been thinking?

Every head turned to look at me when I stepped through the door. I'd grown up in Belle Grove, but it felt like I was a stranger in town now. They looked at me like I was an outsider. I supposed that I was now that I'd been gone for so long. You could never really go home. For a moment I thought about turning around and running out of there, but I figured once these people got an eyeful that they'd go back to their own business. At least that was my plan.

I passed a couple men who were watching me, but I just smiled and nodded as I walked by. After a couple seconds, they offered a half-hearted smile back. That was better than nothing, I guessed. It was too late for me to run away now though. I'd just go to the bar, get my drink and be done. It wasn't like they were going to eat me alive. I just hated being the center of attention.

I approached the bar and took a seat. There was another man sitting at the end of the bar. Other than that, I was alone there.

The bartender approached. He didn't seem to think twice about my presence in the bar.

"What can I get for you?" he asked.

"I'll take a beer," I said.

He nodded and turned around. After a couple seconds he returned with my drink. He placed it down in front of me and I handed him the cash. I took a drink, but couldn't help but feeling that eyes were focused on the back of my head. I grabbed my beer and spun around on the stool, looking out over the crowd. Much to my relief, no one seemed to be watching me now. Thank goodness that was over.

But I knew that I'd felt eyes on me because when I looked across the room, I spotted the men. I recognized one of them. It was Porter Brennan. He was the last person I wanted to see after the way he'd acted at the diner. It made me feel extremely uncomfortable. I took a drink and pretended like I wasn't interested in the fact that the men were watching me. After a couple seconds, I had to look over at them again. They were still watching and I was sure they were talking about me.

Okay, maybe if I turned around they would take a hint and stop watching me. I spun back around and focused my attention on the bottles of liquor on the shelves in front of me. I would take a few more drinks and then just leave. The beer wasn't that good anyway. I should have just gotten chocolate instead. Maybe I could stop by the little store on the corner on my way back to the hotel for a chocolate fix.

I took a couple more drinks and decided that was enough. I'd hung around long enough and it was time for me to get the heck out of there.

Just as the thought had entered my mind, I felt someone walk up to my left and then someone was on my right. When I looked to my left, Porter Brennan had slid onto the stool next to me. His eyes were focused on me. To my right, the other man had taken the other stool. I was now surrounded and my anxiety increased. This wasn't the situation I wanted to be in. I looked straight ahead, as if I ignored them they would go away. I knew that was too good to be true though. They weren't going anywhere.

"How are you this evening?" Porter's words dripped with sarcasm.

I glanced to my left and said, "I'm fine." I didn't ask how he was because right now I really didn't care.

"So what brings you here tonight?"

That was kind of a dumb question. Wasn't it obvious that I was here for a drink?

I avoided looking his way. "Just came for a beer."

He leaned over closer to me. "A pretty girl like you shouldn't be in here all alone."

Gosh, I wanted to push him off that bar stool. Who did he think he was? What a creep. I needed to get out of there. I wondered if I got up to leave if they would try to stop me. I would use the self-defense moves that I'd learned if I had to. He had no right to talk to me this way.

"What brings you back to town?" he asked.

That was none of his business. "I'm from Belle Grove," I said.

"Oh, yeah. Are you here looking for your uncle?" he asked.

I cut a sharp look his way. What did he care if I was looking for my uncle?

He reached over and touched my arm. I yanked my arm away and glared at him.

"Is everything okay here?" the voice said from behind us.

The three of us whipped around all at once. Grant was standing behind us. Was I glad to see him. I guess he'd decided to come for that beer too. Now I was kind of embarrassed that I'd come here. He'd think that I was here for him. That certainly wasn't the case at all. The men glared at Grant.

"We're just having a drink and talking with the young lady." Porter leaned back against the bar and crossed his arms over his chest.

"I wasn't talking to you," Grant snapped.

The men frowned in unison, but didn't say anything in return.

I nodded and said, "I'm fine."

My voice didn't sound so sure though. By the look on Grant's face, he sensed that too. The men turned around and took one last drink from their bottles. Then they stood and walked away, not before giving Grant one last dirty look though. Grant didn't seem to let their glares intimidate him. I'd never seen this tough side of him before.

He met my gaze. "I'll be back in just a moment."

I nodded and watched as he took off toward the men. Whatever happened, I hoped they didn't start a bar fight. I didn't know what I'd do. I couldn't let Grant fight these men alone, but I was pretty sure I would need more than self-defense moves to take part in a bar fight. I envisioned picking up one of those pool sticks and hitting the guy over the head.

Grant followed the men back to the spot where they'd been standing before. He talked with the men, but there wasn't a fight. They didn't look happy with him though. They nodded and then Grant turned and walked back across the bar.

Before Grant had even made it back to the bar, they started walking behind him. I wanted to rush out and push them away. Instead I pointed when Grant looked at me. He turned around and took a defensive stance. The men didn't stop though, instead they continued walking and went out the door without looking back. They hadn't even looked over at me when they left. I wasn't sure what Grant had said to them, but I was glad he did. There was no telling what would have happened if he hadn't shown up.

Grant closed the distance between us and was standing in front of me. "I don't think they'll be bothering you any longer." Oh, wow, my knight in shining armor.

I guessed I should be thankful though, so I said, "Thank you. I don't know what their problem is."

"Do you mind if I sit down?" He gestured beside me.

CHAPTER SIXTEEN

Grant wouldn't tolerate anyone messing with Chloe

Closing the distance between us, I sat on the stool next to her. It was strange being in this setting with her. It was more relaxing, and we were drinking.

"Would you like another drink?" I asked her.

She shook her head. "No, thanks. One is enough for tonight."

The bartender approached and I ordered a beer. Chloe didn't say anything as the bartender came back with my drink. I took a drink and contemplated what I should say. The last thing I needed was to stick my foot in my mouth. I placed my bottle on the counter and looked over at her. She finally looked at me and smiled.

"So what did they say?" I gestured with a tilt of my head.

She shook her head and waved her hand. "They wanted to know why I was in town. I got the impression that they didn't want me here."

That made the hair on the back of my neck stand up. It had sounded a lot like what Gina had said to me. Was there a connection? The man who was with the inspector didn't look anything like the man we'd seen at the office. Besides, Chloe would have recognized him too. I had to tell her about Gina's call.

I took another swig and let the words settle in my mind. Finally, placed the bottle down and said, "There's something I came to tell you."

She quirked a brow. "Oh, yeah? What's that?"

I hated to worry her, but how would I forgive myself if something happened to her and I hadn't shared every detail with her? I couldn't go on knowing that I'd let her down twice. This was my chance to make everything up to her and I was going to give it my best shot. She was staring at me and I knew I had to say something soon.

"Gina called me. She was the call I received when we were together earlier."

Chloe scrunched her brow. "Okay? What's wrong with her?"

"There's nothing wrong with her exactly."

The bartender approached. "Another round?"

Chloe nodded. "Maybe I'd better have another beer after all. Something tells me I'm not going to like what you have to say."

I held up two fingers. "Bring us a couple more."

I took the last swig from my bottle. I knew Chloe's stare was on me and that she wanted to know what I had to say. I was just stalling at this point.

"Are you going to finish telling me about the call?" she asked with frustration in her voice. "What did Gina want?"

"There was a man who approached her earlier today. I think her description of the guy sounded a lot like the one we saw at my office door." I watched for Chloe's reaction.

Her expression darkened. This was a bad sign and I knew right away that Chloe was thinking the worst. How could she not? The bartender brought the beers over and Chloe immediately took a big drink. If she wasn't careful I'd have to carry her out of here. She never could hold her liquor.

I took a drink and then said, "I guess I should remind you that we don't know for sure that this was the same man."

She waved her hand. "Oh, of course it is, that's just the way my luck goes. I wouldn't expect anything less. What did he want?" she asked.

"The man was asking about you. He wanted to know why you were in town and about your uncle too," I said.

"I can't believe you don't know who this man is. I've been gone for ten years so it's understandable that I wouldn't know him, but you should." She pointed her bottle at me.

"Well, the population has doubled in the past few years. If I saw his face I'd probably know who it was."

"So what does that mean?" she asked, then took another big drink.

I watched her pretty face in the light and longed to know what she was really thinking. In one sense it was as if an eternity had passed since I'd seen her, and in another it was as if all those years in between had never happened. I liked having Chloe back and I wished there was a way that she would stay. It wasn't just Chloe's good looks that got me, but her smile, her laugh, her personality, all of it pushed my buttons in a very good way. Her beauty held a sweetness that completely sucked me in.

Finally I said, "I think your uncle didn't leave on his own."

She stared at me for a moment and then said, "I'm glad you finally agree with me. It seems like no one else really cares about him. Other than Gina. I'm just glad she called me when she did."

"I'll help you any way I can."

Chloe offered a little smile. "I appreciate that. What does anyone care if I'm looking for my uncle, anyway? They should have expected that family would come to town if he didn't answer calls."

"Maybe they didn't think he had family since you don't live here anyway."

She looked at me out of the corner of her eye. I'd just reminded her that she'd left town—that was probably not the best choice of words. "What can we do?" she asked, not mentioning what I'd just said.

"I suppose we need to find out who this man is," I said.

"Where do we even start that? Can you ask around town?" she asked.

I nodded. "I'll find out who he is. It's still a small town and I know someone will know him."

"Thanks," she said softly.

"I know your uncle will appreciate that you came all this way to look for him," I said.

Chloe picked at the label on her bottle. "Yeah, well, he's been wanting me to come back to town anyway."

"You didn't want to?" I asked, already knowing the answer.

She didn't look over at me. "I was too busy to come back."

I took another drink. "You've been very busy writing, I see."

"It's what I love to do," she said.

I decided not to pressure her into talking about anything that made her uncomfortable so I steered the conversation back to her uncle.

"I left a message for my brother," I offered.

"What can he do?" she said a little harshly. "I'm sorry," she said immediately after. "I mean, the police didn't seem to want to take it seriously that he didn't leave on his own. So what do you think your brother can do?"

"I understand that you're frustrated, but he'll listen. His hands might be a little tied on what he can do officially, but that doesn't mean he won't help any way that he can," I said.

She nodded. "I truly appreciate it. I don't want to get him in trouble though."

"He'll be fine. Don't worry."

Silence settled over us. I'd been so consumed in our conversation that I'd almost forgotten that we were in the bar surrounded by a lot of people. No one was paying attention to us though. They were all focused with their games of pool and drinks. We drank our beers in silence as I tried to think of what to say next. There was a ton of questions I wanted to ask, but didn't know if she wanted to answer. I felt her glancing over at me several times as if she wanted to speak.

I knew I had to break the silence. Finally, I turned to her and said, "Would you like to go for a walk?"

If she said no then I'd have to walk out of there with my head hung low, but what did I have to lose? The silence had settled over us again and I was having doubts on whether I should have asked. She took a drink from her beer and didn't look over at me. I wondered if she'd even heard me. At that moment I decided I would ask again if she said no.

Just when I was about to ask again she turned to look at me. A little grin slid across her face. "Sure, I'd like that. The smoke in here is getting to me anyway."

I honestly hadn't expected her to say yes, but I was glad that she had.

"Do you want to finish your beer first?" She gestured toward the counter.

"No, it's warm now anyway," I said with a smile.

Chloe grabbed her bag. "Do you think we'll run into those men out there? I think they may have been drunk."

"Don't worry, I won't let them say anything to you."

I pushed to my feet and waited as Chloe stood from her stool. She looked so good in her jeans and tight t-shirt. Her T-shirt clung to her breasts enticingly. Not that I had noticed much. Oh hell, I couldn't take my eyes off her. She was even more beautiful and I hadn't thought that possible. I couldn't help but notice her full lips covered in whatever shiny stuff she'd put on them. She looked over at me and I averted my eyes so she wouldn't think that I was staring. I placed my hand on the small of her back and guided her through the crowd and toward the door. I was glad to get away from the noise and crowd so that we could talk.

Chloe walked along beside me as we headed down the sidewalk. The men were lucky that they hadn't waited around for her. I didn't want to ruin the evening with a fight with them. I was finally getting a chance to spend time with Chloe and I didn't want anything to mess that up.

The smell of something floral and sweet floated over to me. I knew that it was Chloe. Her smell, her smile, her voice, it was all intoxicating and made it hard for me to resist. Did she know what effect she was having on me?

The stars twinkled above in the dark expanse of sky. I couldn't believe that after all this time I was walking next to Chloe. Had the universe brought her back to me? No, I was just being crazy. She'd come back to Belle Grove for her uncle and that was the only reason. As much as I wanted it to be more, I knew that it wasn't. I'd take what I could get though. She was here now and that was all that I cared about. The evening was perfect and I was glad that she'd agreed to let me walk her home.

I had to use this time to talk to Chloe. Discussing why she left or what had happened would be off limits. It would just be general talk about her life now and what she'd been doing. Because honestly, I really wanted to know about her new life in Arizona. There was no need to bring up the past. I wouldn't tell her how much I'd thought about her over the years or how much I'd missed her sweet face.

CHAPTER SEVENTEEN

Chloe should have stopped at one beer

Walking next to Grant felt good. The emotions that seeing him again had brought were totally unexpected. Well, somewhat unexpected. Okay, I had expected them a little. I mean, why else had I stayed away from Belle Grove for so long? I wished I could deny how I felt at the moment, but I couldn't. I still couldn't believe that I'd agreed to let him walk me back to my hotel. But after the confrontation with the men, it was probably the best idea. I liked to think I could take care of myself, but I was no match for two men.

Grant's spicy scent glided across the air and tickled my nostrils. I'd forgotten just how good-looking he was until now. I mean, I'd always remembered, but I thought maybe he'd gotten even better-looking since I'd been gone, with his strong jaw and thick hair. I forced myself to look away so that he wouldn't catch me staring at him. If he caught me I wouldn't be able to hide the desire in my eyes. I wondered what it would be like to kiss him again. Just one kiss and I would probably lose control of my logical thinking skills.

We walked in silence as my thoughts ran a million miles a minute. I wondered what he was thinking and if he felt the same way as me. I'd seen the way he had looked at me a few times. Was it just my imagination? Maybe he was just trying to figure out why the heck I'd come back. Although it seemed that he was beginning to believe me when I said I didn't think my uncle had left on his own. I wished he would say something first so that I didn't have to break the silence.

I felt Grant's tension and noticed that he glanced over at me a few times. Finally, he cleared his throat and said, "I'm glad you came back to Belle Grove."

I had hoped that he would break the silence with a discussion of the weather. I wasn't sure I was ready to talk about my return to Belle Grove.

"Well, I needed to find my uncle, you know."

When I glanced at him I noticed the disappointed look in his eyes. What had he wanted me to say? I wasn't about to admit that I was glad that I'd come back to Belle Grove too.

He nodded. "Yes, I suppose you did need to come back to find him. Is there any other reason you came back? Did you miss the crawfish?"

He offered his dazzling smile and I couldn't help but smile back. "I suppose I did miss that more than I realized."

"It's hard to find in Arizona," he said.

I chuckled. "Yes, it is difficult to locate there."

Silence filled the air again and I figured it was time for me to talk about the weather. Instead, Grant said, "I had decided not to bring this up, but I changed my mind. We should talk about what happened."

I felt his eyes on me. I didn't look over at him. I had to hide my emotions. I had to say something though.

Finally, I settled on, "I don't think we should."

He nodded. "Fair enough, I guess. It's just that the way we left things… and then I don't talk to you again for ten years. You wouldn't answer my calls. Then suddenly you're back in my life and I thought maybe we should talk about what happened."

"I just don't know if this is the right time for this discussion."

Of course I wasn't sure there would ever be a right time. Ignoring something for that long kind of made the topic dead as far as I was concerned. It was buried and that was where we should leave it. Something told me Grant didn't want to leave it buried though.

"I should go. I can walk the rest of the way." Maybe that was a stupid idea, but I could basically see the hotel from there. "Thanks for walking me this far and for taking care of those men." I gestured over my shoulder.

"I've walked you this far. I don't think it would hurt for me to see you to your door."

He had a point, but still, I needed to put distance between us. My feelings were beginning to get away from me and that was something I couldn't let happen. The characters in my books succumbed to romance, but that was fantasy and I was living in the real world. Things like that didn't happen in the real world. In the real world, your boyfriend cheated on you with your best friend. If I wasn't careful, I'd let his dazzling smile get the better of me.

"I appreciate the offer, but I should just go by myself." I didn't give him the chance to say anything else. I stepped away from the curb onto the street. The light was red, but would probably turn green soon, so I hurried my steps. It wasn't like a car would show up because this town was dead after ten. Everyone was either at home or at the bar. I wished I was at home.

Just as the thought left my mind, the engine roared toward me. I'd barely turned my head to the left when I noticed it out of the corner of my eye. It barely had time to register in my mind as the chrome and black rushed toward me.

The roar of the engine filled the night air. My life flashed before my eyes, and let me tell you, I didn't like what I saw. I heard my name called out and the next thing

I knew Grant had grabbed me. He'd jumped from the sidewalk to save me from the car. Grant had risked his life for me.

I didn't know what to think. Of course I would have done the same thing for him. I'd almost been killed. What if Grant hadn't been there? I would have been dead. And to think I'd told him to go away.

When Grant had grabbed me we'd fallen to the pavement. He was still on top of me as my heart raced from the adrenaline.

"Are you okay?" he asked breathlessly.

I nodded and said, "I think I'm okay." I really wasn't sure, though. Nothing hurt but my mind was still in a confused haze.

"Does anything hurt?" Grant stayed on top of me. We were on the road by the sidewalk. The car hadn't even bothered to stop to see if we were okay. I wondered if the driver had even seen me. Surely he had.

"I suppose we should get up," he said.

I couldn't stop staring at his handsome face. "Yes, I suppose we should."

He climbed off me and held out his hand to me. I grabbed it and climbed to my feet. I wiped my hands on my jeans. "Thank you for saving me."

He touched my arm and it was as if an electric jolt ran through me. "Are you okay?"

I nodded and managed to say, "I'm fine. What about you? I think you banged your knee when you hit the ground."

He waved off my comment. "No, I'm fine." He looked up and down the street. "That car came out of nowhere."

I nodded. "I know. I was just thinking how there's never any traffic at this time of night and the next thing I know the car is almost on top of me. I'm just glad you were able to help me." I looked around to see if anyone was watching us. No one was there. This was a crazy thought, but I couldn't help but being suspicious. "Do you think that car tried to hit me on purpose?" I asked. He would probably laugh at my silliness.

He blew out a deep breath and said, "I don't know. I'd like to think it wasn't on purpose." That had me really in a panic. He motioned with a tilt of his head. "Let me walk you to your room."

This time I wasn't going to tell him no. After all, he had saved my life. I hoped that the car wouldn't reappear in the parking lot. I had a feeling it wasn't a coincidence that the car had shown up at that intersection. Plus, I'd had the red light and they hadn't even stopped.

We made our way across the street, but after that I might never cross a street without having a panic attack again. The parking lot was still mostly empty. I looked over at the office and didn't see the woman at the desk. I was glad. I didn't want her to think I was bringing some strange man back to my room. Although it would have been my business if I had. I most definitely wasn't bringing a man back to my room—just Grant Kenner, the man I swore I'd never speak to again. The night air still was humid and I was looking forward to the cool of my room.

We walked across the lot without saying anything. No words were needed at the moment. When we reached the door, I pulled out my key and unlocked the door. A blast of cool air hit me and I relished the feel. I knew what I was going to say next. It wasn't as if it had come to a surprise to me, but I wondered if it would surprise him.

"Do you want to come in?" I asked.

I knew by the look in his eyes that he hadn't expected me to ask. He should know by now that I was full of surprises. No one had ever expected that I would leave Belle Grove, but I had.

I walked through the door and Grant followed. I couldn't lie and say that I wasn't tense about asking him in, but after what had happened, I just wanted someone to talk to right now. I didn't want to be alone. As a matter of fact, I was tired of always being alone. Maybe for one night I could change that. Just for one night. I didn't want to give Grant the wrong impression though and for him to think that we had a chance.

"Would you like a bottle of water?" I asked.

He nodded. "Sure, that would be good. It's still really hot tonight."

I grabbed the bottle of water from the little fridge. "Yeah, I'd forgotten about the humidity, but it only took a few minutes for me to remember."

"I don't want to leave you right now." Grant's gaze was focused like a laser on me.

It was awkward now. What had I thought we would talk about?

"I'm okay by myself." My words didn't sound overly confident.

He took a drink from the bottle and placed it on the table next to the bed. "I'm glad you asked me to come in. I was worried about you after what just happened."

I nodded. "Thanks for caring."

"I've always cared," he said.

I turned my attention away from him. I didn't know what to say. "Would you like to watch the TV?"

He grinned. "Sure."

Maybe I could find a movie that would relieve the tension and the need to talk. It would give me a chance to think of what to say to him. I flipped through the channels until I found a movie. I had no idea what it was, but it didn't matter. Grant leaned back in the chair by the door. He looked uncomfortable as he shifted from one side to the next.

"Why don't you rest and I'll stay for a while?" he said.

How did he know that I didn't want to be alone?

"Would you like to sit on the bed? You can't see the TV from over there." My heart rate increased as the words slipped from my lips.

I knew this was a risky move, but I wanted to be near him. I wanted to smell his masculine scent and feel his strong presence beside me. Grant stared at me for a moment and I felt the electric in his eyes. He walked over to the other side of the bed. He sat back and when I glanced over he offered a sweet smile. I offered a smile back, but I knew that I wanted him to kiss me.

CHAPTER EIGHTEEN

Grant hadn't expected this turn of events

I wouldn't lie and say that I wasn't surprised by what she had done. I hadn't expected her to even talk to me and now I was sitting on the bed next to her. When she'd looked at me I'd gotten a strange feeling that maybe she wanted me to kiss her, but I didn't want to assume and be completely off base. It was probably just wishful thinking on my part.

She laughed at something in the movie and I glanced over at her. The smile on her face sent shivers through my body. She looked so amazing.

The question I kept asking myself was if I should make a move? Right now I was just guessing that she was sending me the message that she wanted a kiss. I didn't want to make an ass out of myself. That was something that I could easily do and would be something that would mess up any chance I had of winning her friendship again. There was only one way to find out how she felt—move in and try to kiss her. Just the thought made my anxiety spike. I wondered if she felt the same way.

As she focused on the movie, I adjusted my body on the bed. I moved a little closer, hoping that she wouldn't notice. I couldn't try to kiss her from the edge of the bed, I would have to be closer. This seemed so ridiculous. If she wanted to kiss she'd probably give me a clear sign. I needed to wait for that sign. Although I realized that it would probably never come. Why did this have to be so difficult? I supposed anything this important wouldn't be easy though. I should have gone after Chloe years ago.

Why had I let her slip away? We were both laughing at the movie now. An easy relaxed feeling had fallen over us. It felt natural to be there with her. As if all those years had never happened. That was just the way that I wanted it. My leg was almost touching hers now. If she noticed she didn't say anything or make any attempt to move away from me. I wanted to touch her hand and caress her skin. Pull her close to my body and hold her tight until the sun came up.

As we continued to watch the movie another funny scene ended with us in laughter. I looked over and Chloe met my stare. This time we didn't turn our attention back to the TV. We stared at each other and I knew that this was my chance to move in for a kiss. If she kicked me off the bed and out of the room, well, that was the chance that I was willing to take. I had been dreaming about kissing her for years and now the time was here. My heart rate increased at the thought of her lips on mine.

Our faces were mere inches apart now and I was glad that she hadn't pulled away. She hadn't kicked me off the bed yet too. She stared at my lips and I was sure that she wanted to kiss me as much as I wanted to kiss her. At least I hoped that I was right. I moved a little closer. That didn't send Chloe running, so I was feeling good about the situation. I couldn't take my eyes off her full lips. My heart thumped as I moved my head closer to hers. She closed her eyes as she leaned in.

I closed my eyes when I placed my lips against hers. I honestly think I stopped breathing for a moment. This was the moment I had been waiting for since she left Belle Grove. Now it was finally here. I gently kissed her and then when she didn't back away, I traced my tongue against her bottom lip. She parted her mouth and my tongue met with hers. My whole body was excited and I didn't want the kiss to stop. Chloe placed her hands along my face and I pulled her close. I was lost in the moment.

I pressed my body closer to hers and felt her full breasts against my chest. She ran her fingers through my hair and I caressed her cheek. I broke free from her kiss and placed my lips softly on her neck. I feathered kisses along her skin working my way down to the exposed skin on her chest. Chloe moved closer and pushed me back on the bed. When I looked into her beautiful eyes, she smiled. She pulled off my shirt and kissed my chest. I closed my eyes and enjoyed the feel of her lips on my skin.

After a few moments of kissing, she smiled and laid her head on my chest. Being with her now was pure bliss and I didn't want the moment to end. I ran my hand through her hair as I listened to her steady breathing. Within a few moments, I knew that she was asleep. I couldn't believe that I was with her and she was peaceful enough to fall asleep. I leaned my head back and closed my eyes. I had my arms wrapped around her. Her warm body felt good against my skin. That was the last thing that I remembered.

*

I woke up to the TV off and only the light from outside the window splashing across the room, causing a strange blue glow across the room. Chloe was no longer lying with her head on my chest. When I glanced over to the other side of the bed, she wasn't there. I sat up in bed trying to focus my eyes. I looked over toward the table and chairs by the window, but didn't see her there either. A panic was starting to settle in. Why was I so upset? She'd probably just gone to the bathroom.

I jumped up from the bed and moved over to the bathroom. Unfortunately, there was no light on in there and the door was open. Clearly, she wasn't in there. I turned around and gave the room another glance. I ran my hand through my hair and released a deep breath. Had she taken off? Maybe my kiss had freaked her out and chased her away. I'd thought that she'd wanted to kiss me too, now I was having second thoughts about whether that had really been the case. Why hadn't she woken me before she had taken off?

I rushed over to the window and took a look outside. The parking lot was still almost empty, although there were a few cars that hadn't been there a few hours ago. Her car was still where she'd left it. Maybe she'd just popped out for a moment. I worried about the men from the bar though. With if they happened to be looking for her? I wasn't sure how she'd gotten out of the room without me waking up. I had to go out there and look for her. Now I really was in a panic.

I eased around the side of the bed and grabbed my shoes. I pushed my feet into them and didn't bother to tie the laces. When I glanced over, her purse wasn't there. I remembered seeing it earlier on the nightstand. So she'd taken her purse, but not her car. She couldn't have gone too far. There was a diner across the street, maybe she'd gone over for a bite to eat. Again, I couldn't understand why she hadn't woken me before she left. I'd never expected to fall asleep and wake up to her being gone.

I went outside and stopped on the sidewalk. I left the door to the room open just a little so that I would be able to get back in if I needed to. Although if Chloe didn't come back there would be no reason why I really needed to be in the room. I looked out over the parking lot and wondered where I should start to look first. I supposed I should take a peek in the car. Maybe she'd gotten in and fallen asleep. Probably unlikely, but I needed to cover all possibilities. Hell, maybe she was just trying to get away from me.

The parking lot was mostly dark in spite of the couple lights around. It was quiet as I expected for three in the morning. There was a light on in the hotel's office. I wondered if Tina was still working. I could ask her if she'd seen Chloe for the second time in just a few hours. She would for sure think I was crazy. I couldn't let that stop me right now though. I didn't care what anyone thought. This had been one hell of a strange evening.

I sprinted across the parking lot and walked into the office. Again no one was in sight until Tina popped up from the back room. She looked at me with a frown again.

"I didn't expect to see you again so soon," she said.

"I didn't expect to be back in here so soon," I said. "I'm looking for Chloe again."

"She seems to keep giving you the slip, huh," Tina said as she moved closer to the front counter.

"We lost each other again," I said, hoping she wouldn't ask for more details.

Tina sat on the stool and leaned her arms on the counter. She looked at me and then pointed across the parking lot. "I saw her walking in the same direction again."

That was the opposite direction from the diner where I had expected that she'd gone. She couldn't have gone to the bar again because it had closed.

"Thank you," I said with a smile.

"I hope you can keep up with her this time," Tina said with a slight chuckle.

I nodded and hurried out of the office. There was only one thing I could do. I had to look for her.

Why would she take off down the sidewalk again? I hoped that car didn't come looking for her again. When I reached the street, I looked in the direction of the diner. I really had thought that she'd probably gone there. I wanted to look in there, but Tina had said that Chloe had walked in the other direction. I had to shake off that feeling though and go with what she had told me. I set off down the sidewalk to find Chloe. I hoped that Tina was wrong and that Chloe was really back in her room and safe.

I walked down the street, looking from side to side, hoping that I would spot her. There was no traffic out at this time of the morning. No people on the streets either. It shouldn't be hard to spot her since no one else was around, although it was dark and even the street lights didn't provide much light. I hadn't decided just how far I would walk before I gave up and went back. There was no telling how long she'd been gone. We'd probably fallen asleep around twelve, so the most she could have been gone was three hours.

I walked a short distance further. But a few steps in front of me I spotted something on the sidewalk. When I neared, I realized that it was a red wallet. I reached down and picked it up. I looked around to see if someone was nearby and had dropped it. No one was in sight, so I opened the wallet. I wasn't expecting what I saw. Chloe's picture was staring back at me. Had she dropped her wallet or had someone stolen it from her and then dropped it here? I decided to go back to her car. I would call my brother and report what I'd found.

CHAPTER NINETEEN

Chloe needs time to wrap her head around what happened

I woke up and realized that I was still lying with my head on Grant's chest. So it hadn't been a dream. What had I been thinking by inviting him in? Silly me for even thinking I could resist him. One flash of his smile and I'd invited him to my room. Thank goodness I hadn't let things go any further.

The soft light from the TV splashed across his handsome face. His chest moved up and down in a steady rhythm. After turning off the television, I slipped out of bed, careful not to wake him. I needed time to think about what had happened.

I eased into my shoes and grabbed my purse. When I reached the door, I looked back at him. He looked so peaceful sleeping there in my bed. For a moment, the thought of seeing him there every night ran through my mind. It was something I could get used to, but I shook off the thought. I needed to put distance between us so that I wasn't influenced by his charm. I'd managed to avoid this for as long as I'd stayed away from Belle Grove, but the moment I was back, I'd fallen right back into his arms.

I was a weak woman.

Fresh air would do me some good and help clear my mind. I eased the door closed and stepped out onto the sidewalk in front of where my car was parked. I decided that I'd just walk over to the little diner, since it wasn't far. Besides, the sound of my car starting might wake Grant. I wanted him to sleep and then I'd come back and talk to him once I'd wrapped my mind around what had happened. I wasn't sure if I'd be able to eat, but I could get some coffee.

As I walked across the parking lot I kept my eyes open for anything strange. I still wanted to know about the man who had been at Grant's office. What had he been doing there? I made it past the hotel's office and I hoped the woman working didn't notice me this time. There were no people out and about at this time of the morning. I was glad that the diner stayed open twenty-four hours though. Visions of Grant sleeping on my bed kept popping back into my mind. A part of me wanted to head right back in there and climb into bed with him.

When I made it to the sidewalk by the main road, I looked to my left and right. That was when I noticed the men down the street. Their backs were facing me, but I recognized them right away. It was Porter Brennan and his sleazy buddy who had harassed me at the bar. There was another man with them too. I hoped that they didn't see me.

I should have run back to the room and grabbed Grant, but that really wasn't an option I wanted to use at the moment. If only I could hear what they were saying.

I decided to walk over that way. Of course I would try my best not to be seen. If they saw me I'd be in big trouble. There was a reason why Porter had told me I should leave town. I bet they knew something about my uncle that they weren't sharing. There was no way I could hide as I walked down the sidewalk toward them. The only thing that saved me at the moment was that their backs were to me. My heart beat quickly as I inched closer and closer toward them. I'd made it pretty darn close to them when they stopped.

They had stopped beside a white car. They still hadn't noticed me, or if they had, they didn't let it be known. I slipped behind a nearby building and peeked around the side. I was officially stalking them now. This was crazy, but after the way they'd acted I figured they deserved it. They shouldn't have made me suspicious of them. I wanted to know what they were talking about in the worst way.

When one of the men turned his face and I saw his profile I realized it was the man who had been at Grant's office. Now I knew I had every right to be suspicious.

Wait until Grant found out about this. He wouldn't be happy. I strained to listen in to their conversation and in spite of the fact that the streets were quiet, I couldn't make out what they were saying. There was no way I could move closer without being seen either. How would I get back down the street without the men seeing me?

I'd barely finished the thought when the men climbed into the car and drove away. Whew. That was lucky. At least now maybe I could make it back to the hotel. But I still hadn't figured out what I would do with Grant.

Maybe now the conversation about these men would be a distraction. I really should go back to the hotel now instead of the diner. I needed to tell Grant about what I'd seen. I inched out from behind the building, looking around to make sure no one was watching me. As I made it down the sidewalk, I dropped my purse and the contents fell out. It was dark and I couldn't see where the things had fallen. My wallet was now missing. Footsteps caught my attention and I scrambled up from the pavement. I raced and hid behind another building.

I had never been this paranoid before. Not only did I have to worry about getting caught by the strange men, but now my wallet was missing and I wouldn't have any money. What would I do now? The footsteps continued near the building, but then they stopped. I wanted to peek out, but I was afraid to. Finally, the footfalls sounded again and faded from my ears. I eased my head around the building. That was when I saw him. At least I thought for sure it was Grant. What in the heck was he doing? He would probably ask me the same thing.

I jumped out from around the building and took off after Grant. So much for having time to think about what I was going to say to him. If he asked about the kiss I'd tell him that it was a momentary lapse in judgment and that nothing like that could ever happen again. It would be the best for both of us. There had just been too much time between us to make up for the lost time. Sometimes you just had to let the past stay in the past. There was no sense in stirring up the old wounds.

When I made it out onto the sidewalk, Grant had already made it a good distance away. It would take running for me to stand a chance of catching up to him. I threw my big purse over my shoulder and took off in a sprint. This bag wasn't exactly made for running, especially since I had the kitchen sink in it. A girl never knew when she might need lip balm or bandages.

Grant didn't even know that I was behind him. I was glad that he hadn't looked back and seen my awful display of running. An athlete I was not.

I was shocked that he hadn't heard my heavy breathing when I made it all the way behind him. I was so close now that I could reach out and touch him and that was exactly what I did. When I tapped him on the shoulder, he jumped and then spun around. His arms were up in defense. I held my hands up in surrender.

"It's just me," I said.

He lowered his hands. "What are you doing?"

Telling him that I'd been out for a casual stroll wouldn't be an option. Of course he probably knew that I'd freaked out about what had happened between us. Could he really blame me though?

I guessed I would have to tell him the truth. "I decided to go to the diner for something to eat. I woke up and was hungry." That wasn't a lie, I had been going to the diner.

He frowned. "The diner is in the opposite direction."

Yes, there was that. "I didn't make it to the diner."

"I can see that."

"When I got out to the street I noticed Porter Brennan and the other man from the bar. I wanted to know what they were doing."

"That is dangerous. What if they'd harassed you again?"

I shrugged. "I didn't say it was a good plan."

"I'm guessing they didn't see you," he said.

I shook my head. "No, I don't think they did. But the man who we saw at your office was with them."

"Are you sure?" he asked.

I nodded. "I'm almost positive. They left in a white car."

He ran his hand through his hair. "I was worried about you." He held out my red wallet.

"My wallet! Where did you find it?" I asked.

"It was on the sidewalk. Of course you can understand why I assumed the worst. Please don't ever do that to me again." He stared me straight in the eyes.

As far as I was concerned there wouldn't be a chance for me to do it again. I was leaving as soon as I found my uncle. I didn't bother telling Grant that right now though. I had to worry about finding my uncle. Grant would figure out when I was gone that I had no intention of having a relationship with him. I took the wallet from his outstretched hand.

"As long as you're okay now," he said.

I nodded. "I'm fine."

He stared at me and I knew he wanted to ask why I had left. Luckily, he didn't. Grant motioned with a tilt of his head. "Let's go for breakfast."

I stared at him.

"You were going there anyway, right?" he asked.

I nodded. "Yes, I remembered it has been a while since I ate."

"We can discuss what happened… with the men."

I was glad that he added that last part. If I steered the conversation toward my uncle then I hoped to avoid the other topic entirely. I stuffed my wallet back in my bag.

"I thought you'd been mugged or kidnapped," he said.

I nodded. "I dropped my purse. I suppose I wouldn't make a great spy."

"Probably not," he said with a chuckle.

We started off down the sidewalk in silence. If I wasn't careful he would be talking about what had happened at the hotel. I needed to start some kind of conversation. Luckily, it wasn't a long walk to the diner. I could see the place from where we were on the street.

"So how did you know where to look for me?" I asked.

He smiled. "Tina at the office saw you go this way."

"She watches what's going on, huh?" I said.

He laughed. "Nothing gets by her."

I'd have to thank her for that later.

We made it to the diner and Grant held the door open for me. There was not another soul in the place.

"Sit anywhere you'd like," the waitress said without looking at us.

"How about the booth right there?" Grant pointed.

"Sure." I slid onto the booth just as the waitress brought over a couple of menus.

I ordered juice and Grant had a cup of coffee. The booth a couple back from us was where I'd seen the inspector. I wondered if the same waitress was here this morning. I glanced around but didn't see her.

After placing our orders, Grant looked at me. "So we know that the man from my office is connected to the inspector and the other man. I plan on paying Porter a visit in just a few hours. I want to know what the man was doing."

I took a drink of my juice. "I have a feeling he won't tell you anything."

"Maybe not, but I think I'll take my brother along to see what they have to say to that."

Grant looked so handsome sitting across from me and I wanted another kiss. What was I thinking? A kiss wasn't a part of my plan.

CHAPTER TWENTY

Grant wants to forget about the past

After eating, I walked Chloe outside and back to her room.

"Why didn't you tell me about your writing? You never said you wanted to be a writer, and the next thing I know you've got bestselling books on the shelves," I said.

"I didn't know at the time, but I'm glad I figured it out."

"I'm glad too." I fought the urge to hold Chloe's hand as we strolled along.

"I knew what you would be doing. You've always been out there on that bayou." A smile quirked the corners of her too sensual lips.

I shoved my hands into my pockets. "It wasn't much of a surprise, was it?"

"How long ago did you buy your house?" she asked.

"About six years ago. I thought if I bought the house next to your uncle that you might come for visit."

She looked at me out of the corner of her eye, but didn't respond.

"What kind of place do you have in Arizona?" I asked.

"It's a nice little apartment. The place is kind of like a retirement community. I'm the youngest one there. But there's great places to eat and shop right around the corner."

"I know a great place to shop right here in Belle Grove. I happen to know the owners quite well." I smiled.

Chloe chuckled. "I still can't believe your mother tried to play matchmaker."

"She would be happy if she saw us talking."

I wasn't sure how it had happened, but she had successfully avoided talking about what had happened in the room and our past. In spite of all that, it was a great conversation as we talked about what we were doing in our current lives.

When we reached the room's door, she turned to me and said, "Well, thanks for everything."

I couldn't take my eyes off her sweet face. Maybe she wouldn't talk about what had happened, but that wouldn't stop me from kissing her again. I reached out and pulled her close, planting a kiss right on her mouth.

For a moment she acted as if she would pull away, but then she kissed me back. Her mouth moved across mine and I didn't want the moment to end. Finally, she pulled away and stared me in the eyes.

"I'd better go," she said.

As she turned and walked through the door, I said, "I'll call you."

She nodded as she faced me again. Without saying another word, she closed the door. Well, that was progress. At last she hadn't told me never to call her again. I walked away, but when I'd made it halfway across the lot, I looked over my shoulder.

Chloe had the curtain pulled back and was watching me. She pulled the curtain shut quickly as I smiled. When I climbed behind the wheel of my truck, I pulled out my cell phone. It rang several times and then my brother finally picked up.

"What the hell are you calling so early for?" he asked.

"I think something is going on," I said.

"Don't be enigmatic. Tell me what's up."

"Porter Brennan and some other dude was harassing Chloe last night."

"Well, I'm not surprised, the guy is a creep."

"Yeah, well, some other dude he was talking to was messing around at my office," I said.

"What did you say to him?" he asked.

"I didn't catch him to say anything, but I'd like a chance to."

Ty chuckled. "I guess that's where I come in."

I turned the truck's ignition. "That's the plan, yes."

"As soon as he's in the office we'll go talk with the inspector."

After telling him where to find me, I leaned my head back on the truck's seat and waited. I closed my eyes, but all I saw was Chloe's sweet face. I needed to focus on other things and not let myself get wrapped up with a fantasy that she was going to stay around Belle Grove.

Once her uncle was back in town, she would be gone. If only there was a way for me to get her to stay. Where did we go from here?

I was startled by a horn honking from behind me. I opened my eyes and looked in the rear-view mirror. Apparently I'd tossed off because it was now eight in the morning. Ty was in his police cruiser behind me. He motioned for me to get in.

I climbed into the passenger seat.

"What's the plan?" he asked.

'I want to find out who this man is who was messing around my office."

"Why didn't you go after him?" Ty asked.

"I did, but I guess he got away. Chloe had seen a boat with a few men on it earlier. I think that's how he got away."

Ty tapped his fingers against the steering wheel. His police radio crackled in the background. "I think the best place to start is if we pay the inspector a visit."

I nodded. "He told Chloe that she should leave town and I want to find out why he would say that. What does he care if she's in town? He doesn't know her."

"Unless he's done something with her uncle and he's afraid she'll find out."

I released a deep breath. "I didn't want to say it, but yeah, that's what I'm afraid of."

"Look, maybe we'll be wrong," Ty said.

"There's only one way to find out," I said.

He started the car and we pulled out onto the road. As we made our way down Main, I glanced over at the hotel parking lot. Chloe's car was still parked in the same spot. I hoped that she would be okay. Ty parked his car in front of the building which housed the inspector's office.

Ty knocked on the door. "Go away," Porter said from the other side.

"Belle Grove Police," Ty replied in a stern voice.

Noise sounded from the other side and then the door opened. When the inspector saw us he said, "What do you want?"

"Now is that any way to talk to your old friend from the police department?" Ty said.

Porter snorted and walked across the room. "Old friend, my ass."

"I guess we'll invite ourselves in," I said.

He sat at his desk and looked us up and down. "To what do I owe this pleasure?" he quipped.

Ty and I sat in the chairs in front of his desk. "Why don't you tell him why we're here," Ty said without looking at me.

I leaned back and stared at Porter for a moment. "Why were you harassing Chloe Beaumont last night?"

Porter chuckled. "Hell, I knew you'd be in there today asking me that. We had too many drinks. We were just having some fun. She must have taken what we said the wrong way."

That was a pathetic excuse and I knew he was full of crap. "Who was the guy you were talking to last night?"

"That's Frank. He works for me," he said.

"No, not at the bar. The man you were talking to early this morning. You drove away with him in a white car," I said.

"Are you following me?" he asked.

I shook my head. "No, not following you. Just doing a little research. See, we like to know what's going on in Belle Grove too, don't we, Ty."

Ty nodded. "Yep."

"I don't know who you're talking about."

"So you didn't drive away in a white car this morning with two other men?" I asked.

He shook his head, but avoided my stare. "Nope, I was at home. Some of us like to get our beauty sleep, you know."

"It's not working," Ty quipped.

Porter laughed. "So I've been told."

I crossed my arms in front of my chest. "I don't think you're being honest with us."

"Why don't you tell us where to find this guy?" Ty asked.

Porter leaned back and glared at me. "I told you I don't know who you're talking about."

"Look, we know he was trying to break into Grant's office last night. If we have to hunt him down then it could be bad for you too," Ty said.

"Is that a threat?" He continued to glare at us.

Ty shook his head. "No, not a threat, just a fact."

Porter tapped his fingers against his desk. "If I find out who it is, then I'll be sure to let you know. Now is there anything else I can do for you all?"

"I take it you won't be bothering Chloe anymore?" I asked.

He stared for a moment longer and then offered a fake smile. "No, of course not, and if I upset her I'm truly sorry. Please offer my sincere apologies."

I nodded as I pushed to my feet. I wished I could get the truth out of this guy, but it didn't look as if it was going to be that easy. I would get to the bottom of it though.

"Thanks for the visit now," he said as we walked out the door.

"What do you think?" I asked as we made our way back to Ty's car.

"Yeah, he's full of it. I'll ask around and see what I can find out."

"There's something to this disappearance and I have a feeling this guy knows what that is. Chloe mentioned that her uncle's card had been used recently."

"Can you get me that info?" Ty asked.

"I'll see what I can find out," I said.

For Chloe's sake I hoped she found her uncle soon. Although the closer we got the worse I felt about not seeing her again.

"I've not liked that guy for as long as I can remember. Hell, the day he showed up in town I knew he was trouble," Ty said.

"You think he's lying?" I asked.

"I know he's lying," Ty said. "I just need to find a way to prove it."

"Yeah, and find out why. What was the connection between her uncle and him?"

"I'll look into that too. You should talk to Anna Louise at the diner. She dated him for some time," he said. "I bet Porter will be in the bar again tonight. Maybe I should check it out."

"It couldn't hurt to try," I said. "Maybe I'll come with you."

Ty cast a glance over at me. "You think Chloe will be there?"

I ignored his question. "I think he knows about her uncle. I won't stop until I find out the truth."

"I've never seen you so persistent before," he said.

"I guess it's my way of making up for the past."

He nodded. "I can understand that. You did mess things up with her pretty good. You let a good thing go. She looks good and seems just as sweet as I remember."

He wasn't making me feel better. But I couldn't deny that he was being honest.

"So how do I find out what's going on?" I wanted to steer the conversation away from Chloe.

He looked at his watch. "I need to get to work, but I'll ask around and let you know. In the meantime, I'm going to look into what he's been doing."

"I appreciate that. I can't guarantee that I won't check him out on my own," I said.

"What do you mean? Don't cause more problems. I don't need you in jail for assaulting this guy."

"Hey, what do you think I am? I wouldn't do anything to him unless provoked."

Ty stared for a beat and then said, "Yeah, my guess is he'll do something to provoke you."

I shrugged. "The man has an attitude. That tells me that he's guilty of something."

"Well, it tells me that he's just an asshole," Ty said.

"Yeah, that too."

I opened the car door and got out. He opened the passenger side window. "I tried to call you last night. Is that when you were at the bar?"

I nodded. "Probably."

"It was kind of late though. I'm surprised you didn't hear your phone." He quirked a brow.

"What are you getting at?"

"Are you sure the bar is the only place you went last night? Did you spend some time with Chloe?"

"None of your business," I said.

"You might as well come clean with me," he warned.

"Yeah, I'll make sure to do that." I didn't want him reminding me of my past mistakes so there was no reason to share the latest developments with him.

"Make sure you keep an eye on Chloe." He smiled. "But I guess I don't need to tell you that, huh? I guess you've got that covered."

I shook my head and walked off. I knew I would hear the end of this from him. He'd always given me attitude for losing her.

Flashes of Chloe ran through my mind and I knew I had to find her uncle and the reason why the inspector was telling her to leave town. But where would I start? Since I had the day off, I knew I had time to poke around town. I'd head home and jump in the shower, then head out and see what I could find out. Maybe I'd stop in and check on Chloe too. We could grab some lunch and discuss the situation… and I could catch another kiss.

CHAPTER TWENTY-ONE

Chloe needed to erase Grant from her mind

I couldn't believe what Grant had done. Yes, secretly I was glad that he'd swooped me up in a big kiss, but I couldn't let him know that. How long would I continue to ignore the elephant in the room? I wouldn't be able to keep this up forever if I stayed in Belle Grove for much longer. That was why I needed to get out of there soon.

Of course that brought me back to the main problem: I needed to find my uncle. I was no closer to finding him than when Gina had first called me.

Ignoring Grant wouldn't be an option, so I'd have to just deal with him until I left. No more kisses though. I'd have to keep my distance. I guessed going to breakfast with him had probably given him the wrong impression. I appreciated his help, but it just made matters worse. I didn't need to fall in love again and just have my heart broken. Life was much easier without dealing with that kind of pain. I'd let the characters in my novels deal with those kind of problems. It was their story, not mine, and that was the way I wanted it to stay.

There was one thing I hadn't figured out though. Why was Grant helping me? He certainly didn't have to. After all this time he couldn't have acted as if he'd never seen me. I had ignored his calls for the first year and then he'd given up, so why now was he trying to help me? Maybe I was being too suspicious and maybe there was no motive other than just being nice. Of course I could just come right out and ask him, but I figured that would bring up the topic I wanted to avoid.

I looked over at the bed where he had been lying just a short time ago. I shook off the thought. I'd jump in the shower, slip into a change of clothing, and then take off for a little poking around. With any luck, I'd find something that would help me find my uncle.

After stepping out of the shower, I pulled on a pair of denim shorts and a black T-shirt. Then I slipped on my sneakers and pulled my hair back into a pony tail. It was going to be another hot day and I knew the humidity would get the best of my hair.

As much as it made me sad to go back to my uncle's place, I decided to give it another try. At least I could look around again to find something that might lead me to his whereabouts.

Every time I drove down his street I had to look over at Grant's. It was like an accident and I couldn't look away. This time I tried my best not to look over, but as I passed his driveway I couldn't control it and I glanced over. At least it was just a quick glance though. I wasn't sure, but I didn't see his truck in the driveway.

After parking the car I made the small walk up the path and to my uncle's front door. Just a short time ago I had been there with Gina. I opened the door and stepped into the dim space. Although it was daytime, the space never got much sun because of all the surrounding trees. I flipped on the switch in the hallway and flooded the room with light. It looked the same as the other day when I'd been there, but of course I knew that it would.

Now that I was back I had no idea what I was looking for or where to look for it. I would just start with the living room and then work my way through the rest of the house. I stepped over to the living room and gave a quick glance around the room. Beige walls without any pictures made for a bland room. There wasn't much there or many places to store stuff so I moved on to the kitchen/dining room. I shifted through the papers on the table, but only found receipts and bill stubs. There were a few dirty dishes in the sink and I wanted to wash them. There was no time right now though.

I remembered seeing papers in his office, so I decided to head to that room next. I was beginning to feel this was a wasted trip though. It was hard not to get discouraged after this much time with no leads to my uncle's whereabouts. I moved down the dimly lit hallway and took a peek in the bedroom first before going across the hall to the office. I wanted to make his bed and put away the clean laundry he'd left on the bed, but like the dishes, there was no time. Next I moved over to the office.

I stepped into the room. It was a little lighter in there since the sun was shining at the front of the house and bouncing in the windows at the front of the room. I stood in the middle of the room and placed my hands on my hips. Where to start? There was a file cabinet and a desk, so I decided to look through the desk first.

I rooted around in the desk but didn't notice anything different from the last time I was in there. I was just about to give up when I glanced to my left and saw a cassette tape. I hadn't seen one of those in years since I listened to my mother's Madonna cassette. I placed it back on the desk and continued to look through the desk. I still hadn't found anything so I moved over to the file cabinet. I looked through each cabinet but the files were mostly empty. I turned around and released a deep breath.

That was when my eyes traveled back to the cassette tape on the desk. There was something written on it that I hadn't noticed before. I stepped back to the desk and picked up the tape. It had the inspector's name written on it. That was really odd. Why would my uncle have a tape with Porter Brennan's name written on it? This definitely had me curious and only added to the mystery. I had to know what was on that tape. I stuffed the tape in my pocket and headed out the door back into the hallway.

How would I get this thing to play? I didn't have a tape player and I didn't know anyone who had one either. Did they even sell them anymore? Would I find one at the antique store? I turned back around and into the office. He had to have a tape player somewhere in the house. The first place to look would be in his office. It would probably be somewhere near where he'd had the tape. Unfortunately the player wasn't near the tape. I looked through the rest of the room but couldn't find the player anywhere.

After checking everywhere else in the house that I could think of I realized that there was no player there. How had he listened to the tape? Had he listened to it? If he had it then why would he have not listened to it? I would have to find a player somewhere. My uncle had to have a player, but I'd given up on finding it. There was a Walmart in town and I prayed that I could find one there. If they didn't have one then who would? I'd have to ask around town to see who had one. Surely someone would. I wondered if the inspector knew if my uncle had taped him. Was that what the tape was? It was the only logical thing I could think of.

I'd just made it across the floor and to the front door when I heard noise. It sounded like someone was outside the door. My heart rate increased. I peeked out the window and saw Grant headed toward the door. Damn. He'd obviously seen my car but I didn't want to talk to him. Would it be immature of me to hide from him? Probably but that wasn't going to stop me from doing it. I'd already said that I had issues. This was one of them.

I ran over the living room, almost tripping over the coffee table. I cussed as I limped over toward the sofa. The door opened and I knew that he was coming inside. Not that I had doubted that but now it was being confirmed. There was no place for me to hide really. The only place I had to duck was behind the sofa. So that was exactly what I did. I knelt down and tried to steady my breathing so that he wouldn't hear me. The door opened and I held my breath, wondering if he could see me.

I peeked out from behind the sofa. Grant stood there looking down the hallway. He hadn't called out to me yet. But that was when he said, "Chloe?"

Then I realized that I was being ridiculous hiding from him like a little kid. I had to come out and let him know what I was there. He still had no idea that I was hiding behind the sofa. If he turned around he would see me peeking out at him like a fool. What had I been thinking? I had to stop this craziness.

I stepped out from behind the sofa and walked toward Grant. He still hadn't turned around and noticed me. He'd inched further into the kitchen area, so I went after him. I was just glad that he hadn't seen me hiding behind furniture. Now I could pretend that had never happened. By the time I caught up, he'd moved all the way into the kitchen. I was surprised that he hadn't heard my footsteps trailing him.

Grant looked dashing today as usual and I hated that I was actually thinking about his looks. There were clearly more important things. When I was right up behind him, I gripped his shoulder. "What are you doing here?"

He spun around as if he was confronting a burglar. I was probably lucky that he hadn't instinctively punched me.

"You scared the hell out of me," he said with his hands still up in defense.

"Sorry."

"I saw your car and wondered if everything was okay."

Yeah, I didn't believe that story. He had to have driven down here first before even seeing my car. "Everything's fine, but I found this tape." I pulled the cassette from my pocket.

He took it from my hand. "What do you think it is? Is it important?"

"Look at the back." I pointed.

He flipped it over and then met my stare.

I nodded. "Exactly. Why else would it have Porter's name on it?"

"So you think this is something your uncle secretly recorded?"

"That's what I have to find out. But I don't have a way to play it. I looked all over the house for a player."

He grabbed my hand. "Come on, we'll buy a tape player."

I couldn't believe that I was back in the truck with Grant again. How did I continually end up with him? He tapped his fingers against the wheel as he steered.

"Are you wondering what is on that tape too?" I asked.

He nodded. "Yeah, I'm a little curious. This could be exactly what we need to find your uncle."

I released a deep breath. I hoped what he said was right. Another disappointment was the last thing that I wanted.

"Now we just have to hope that we find a way to play the tape."

"We'll find a way, don't worry," he said.

CHAPTER TWENTY-TWO

Grant was thankful for an excuse to be with Chloe

I pulled into the first available space and shoved the truck into park. We jumped out at the same time. Chloe didn't even give me a chance to help her out of the truck. I couldn't blame her; I wanted to know what was on the tape too. The store was mostly empty with only a couple employees at the registers. Chloe practically ran back to the electrics department.

"I hope they have one," she said over her shoulder.

"Wait for me," I said.

When we made it to the correct aisle, she stopped and placed her hands on her hips. "I don't see anything. What will we do now?" Chloe sounded as if she was about to panic.

I spotted one in front of me, but didn't tell her. I wanted a chance to find another one before I pointed the pink one out.

"Right there," she said, pointing to the Disney Princess sing-a-long cassette player.

I reached down and grabbed the box. "Disney Princess it is. Just don't tell my brothers."

"If you're good I'll let you have it." Chloe chuckled. Her laughter was music to my ears.

When we reached the register I realized the woman working, Paige, was friends with Ty. So much for not telling my brothers.

Paige looked down at the pink box. "Birthday gift?"

I grabbed the box. "Yeah, that's it. Birthday gift."

"Is that all for you?" Paige asked.

Chloe grabbed a package of chocolate chip cookies from the display near the register and placed them on the counter. "I'll need these for later."

"Tell Ty I said hello," Paige said as we walked away.

Chloe was still laughing about the pink princess cassette player as when we reached the truck. I was glad that this had relieved her tension for a couple minutes. I'd sacrifice my ego in order for Chloe to feel better. I pulled the cassette player out of the box while Chloe unpackaged the batteries. I shoved the batteries in and we were all set.

"I've got the tape," she said, pulling it from her purse.

After slipping the cassette into the slot, I pushed play and then held my breath waiting to hear the mysterious message. With our luck the tape would be blank, only adding to the puzzle surrounding her uncle.

Chloe fidgeted with her hands as the sound came from the speakers. There was movement as if someone was walking and then Taylor's voice.

"I came to ask you one last time if you're going to do the right thing," Taylor said.

I recognized the next voice right away.

Porter Brennan said, "I told you what I need in order to get it done."

"So you're blackmailing me? Is that the way you do all business around here?" The anger in Taylor's voice was evident.

There was more movement, and then Porter said, "We're through here."

"Oh, so you're going to shoot me?" Taylor asked.

I glanced at Chloe. She looked as if she might be ill.

"Fine, I'm leaving. Don't touch me," Taylor said.

It was then that the tape shut off. I pushed eject and took the tape out of the player. I was glad the tape had cut off because I didn't want Chloe to have to endure any more of it. This would only increase her suspicions that her uncle had met with some serious trouble, and rightfully so.

Chloe placed her head in her hands. "He has to have done something to my uncle."

I touched her hand. "We'll find out."

Chloe leaned her head back against the truck's seat. "My uncle used to pick me up every Saturday when I was young and we would go out junking, as he called it. I brought home so much random junk, it probably drove my mother crazy. But we had so much fun."

I laughed. "Your uncle likes a bargain."

"That's a nice way of saying he likes random junk." She chuckled.

Chloe wiped her cheeks and a silence settled over us. I didn't want to interrupt her thoughts until she was ready to talk.

"Can you take me back to my car?" Chloe asked.

I didn't want to leave her in this condition, but what other choice did I have?

CHAPTER TWENTY-THREE

Chloe searches for a clue

Grant asked me to come back to his place when he dropped me off at my car, but I figured that wasn't anything I needed to do right now. I wanted to go to the police right away with the tape. Grant had called his brother and told him about the tape. He said they would come by and pick it up. Maybe then they'd open a missing person case on my uncle.

In the meantime I was going to try everyone else I could think of to find Uncle Taylor. I had the name and address of the hotel that had been charged to his card recently. Even though I was anxious about what I might discover, I picked up the phone and dialed the number. It would be a long shot, but maybe someone there would remember him.

After a couple rings, a woman answered, "Orange Hill Inn. How may I help you?"

"Good evening. My name is Chloe Beaumont. I wonder if you can help me locate someone who stayed at your hotel."

There was silence on the line.

"Hello?" I said.

"I don't think I can help you with that information," she said.

Before she could hang up, I rushed my words. "My uncle is missing and he stayed at your hotel. You don't have to tell me what room he is in, just if you saw anyone with that description. Please."

"I really don't think I'm supposed to do that."

"Please. It's important that I find him. This is the only clue I have to his possible whereabouts."

If she said no then I had no clue what I would do next. My options were exhausted.

Finally, she sighed and said, "Okay, but this is off the record. Don't tell anyone I gave you information."

It would be a long shot that she would have even seen him.

"Thank you. I appreciate your help. His name is Taylor Beaumont and there was a charge from this hotel. He is tall with dark hair. He always wears shorts and polo shirts."

"Oh yeah, I remember him." There was excitement in her voice, which made me excited too.

"So he was there," I said.

"He was here the other day, but he checked out. I think it was yesterday."

Of course that made my heart sink. I left her my contact information to call me if he returned. Why had he taken off? I doubted whether this woman was truly sure that it was my uncle that she'd seen. But her information had given me new hope that we would find my uncle alive. Was someone with him? I should leave tomorrow to go to that hotel. There was no way that I would tell Grant that I was leaving though.

CHAPTER TWENTY-FOUR

Grant might be on to something

I needed to talk with Anna Louise. If she dated the inspector maybe she could give me information. It could lead nowhere and it probably would, but I'd give it a shot anyway.

I drove the short distance to the diner. The parking lot was mostly empty, which would give me more of a chance to talk with her. After parking the truck, I hopped out and hurried across the parking lot. The diner was close to Belle Grove Inn and I wondered what Chloe was doing. I had to shake off the thought. The more I thought about her, the more I was building myself up for disappointment.

When I stepped in the door, I scanned the area. A couple people I knew were sitting in the corner of the diner, so I tossed my hand up that way and then sat at the counter by the register. I grabbed a menu and pretended to look it over as if I didn't know every single item on it already. It hadn't changed much in all the years I'd been coming in. I spotted Anna Louise in the kitchen, but she hadn't noticed me yet. I continued to look over the menu and finally decided that I wasn't going to eat anyway, so I'd just order a water. And maybe a slice of apple pie.

Out of the corner of my eye, I spotted Anna Louise headed my way, so I dropped the menu and smiled at her.

She returned the expression as she grabbed her coffee pot. "Do you want some coffee?"

I didn't have the heart to say no now that she'd flipped the mug over and already poured half a cup. "Thanks," I said as I grabbed the sugar.

Anna Louise seemed quiet today and I wasn't sure that I would be able to get her to talk. She set the pot down and turned to face me. "Are you ready to order?" She placed her hands on her hips and stared at me, making me have second thoughts about only ordering the pie. Maybe if I left a bigger tip she wouldn't be angry with me.

"Can I get a slice of apple pie and a glass of water?"

She picked up a few plates from the counter and said, "You want ice cream with that?"

"No, I'll skip the ice cream today."

"All right, coming up." She spun around again without giving me a chance to say another word.

Somehow I would have to get her to hang around long enough for a conversation. After a couple seconds she placed the slice on the plate and then prepared my glass of water.

She set the plate in front of me. "What else can I get you?"

I grabbed the fork. "This looks delicious. Did you make the pie?"

I sank my fork into the crust and cut off a chunk. She stared at me for a moment and then snorted.

"No, we buy it prepackaged. There's not much that's homemade here in the diner."

"Why does the sign say homemade pie?"

She shrugged. "I suppose it's homemade by someone."

I couldn't argue with that.

"So can I get you anything else?" she asked.

I finished chewing my bite and then said, "I want to ask you about Porter Brennan."

Her expression changed and she looked around. "What do you want to know about him?"

"Well, excuse me if this is too personal, but didn't you date him for a while?"

"That is a personal question," she snapped.

I nodded. "I'm sorry, I just wanted to know more about him."

"What do you want to know?"

"He's been in town for a while and I don't know much about him. He's not the friendliest guy around."

"Porter is okay." She wiped off the counter, but I knew she was avoiding my stare.

"He's been trying to talk with my friend Chloe. I want to know why he would want her out of town. Do you know anything about that?"

Anna Louise's face had turned pale. "I don't know why he would want anyone out of town. He's always nice to everyone."

"Yeah, I haven't been witness to any of his pleasantries."

Anna Louise didn't deny it and I knew that she agreed with me. "Why don't you ask him?"

"He's not really answering my calls right now. I'm not his favorite person," I said.

She stopped wiping down the counter and looked me in the eyes. "Porter helps a lot of people in town."

I knew she wasn't telling the truth with that one. "What kind of help?" I asked.

"Like when they need help with the building process," she said smugly.

I shrugged. "Maybe so, but that's not what I'm worried about. I just need to know why he's so hostile toward Chloe."

She poured more coffee into my almost full mug. "I thought you two weren't friends anymore."

I stared at her. "You heard wrong."

Anna Louise shrugged. "She seems like a nice girl. If only she wasn't hanging around Gina."

"What do you mean by that? What problem do you have with Gina?" I asked.

She shook her head. "Never mind."

I finished off the last of the pie. "So who are the other men Porter has been hanging around with?"

"I'm not his keeper, how should I know who he's with?"

"I just thought you might have seen him with the men lately. They seem to be spending quite a bit of time together. What's their relationship?"

I had to find out who the man was we'd seen that night at my office. There had to be a reason why they were acting so mysterious and secretive. Getting answers from Anna Louise wasn't easy though. It would be easier to get an answer from the glass of water in front of me.

"Like I said, I don't know who they are. I haven't seen him talking with anyone lately." She quickly looked away.

I was getting closer to getting something from her and I couldn't give up now. I would press her for more info. "He has been in several places around town with these men."

She waved her hand. "Sorry. I don't know what to tell you. How about another slice of pie?" She smiled widely.

The pie wasn't going to make me stop asking her questions. It was good, but it wasn't that good.

"I don't believe what you're telling me, Anna Louise. So why don't you just be honest with me? Why are you trying to hide something from me?"

She scowled. "Look, I don't you I don't know anything. Besides, even if I asked him he wouldn't tell me anything. He'd just tell me to mind my own business."

"Porter sounds like a great guy. Why would you even talk to him?"

"He has his good qualities," she said, filling my glass with water again. I couldn't imagine that was possible. She was just trying to make excuses for him. "He won't tell me anything. He's helped me a lot though, so I owe him my friendship."

I frowned. "What is that supposed to mean? You mean he is buying your friendship?"

"Of course not," she snapped.

"Then what do you mean?"

"He's loaned me money when I needed help and no one else would. I just think he deserves my friendship because of that."

"I don't think that's true if he's not nice to you," I said.

She looked down.

"Why don't you tell me the truth?"

"Why should I talk to you?"

"Because I will truly be your friend."

She sighed and then finally looked at me. "I can't get away from him."

"What do you mean?" I asked.

"It's just like I said, he helped me and now I have to help him."

"What do you have to help him with?"

"Anything he wants. Sometimes I just run errands for him. Sometimes I just offer him my friendship."

I wasn't sure exactly what she was talking about. But it sounded odd and not like a normal friendship. Not like a friendship I'd heard of before.

"Does he bully you?" I asked.

She picked up my plate. "No."

Something in her eyes told me that wasn't the case. The more I heard about this guy the less I liked him. I wasn't sure I even wanted to hear more. I'd heard plenty. So he was used to getting favors for money. I wondered if he did that with everyone.

"I heard he likes the ladies. You know, he has a lot of dates."

That made her face turn red. "That's not true. Who told you that?"

I took a drink of water and then said, "It's just the rumor around town."

"Well, it's not true." She glanced around the room. "I can't talk anymore right now."

"Do you mind if I come back to talk later?" I asked.

"There's nothing else to say," she said.

I leaned back on the stool. "Oh, I don't know. Something tells me that I will find something else to talk about."

She scowled. "You can do whatever you want." She placed the ticket next to me on the counter.

I fished out a few bills and laid them next to my glass. "Great. Thanks again for the pie, even if you didn't make it."

She shook her head. "Whatever."

I watched as she walked away. She probably knew that my eyes were still on her. I wanted to know what kind of jobs she had done for Porter. How many other people did he have doing jobs for him? That was probably his connection to the other men. It seemed like I would have a difficult time finding out though. Anna Louise wasn't willing to share much and everyone else would probably be that way too. I'd ask Ty what he knew about this situation. Although if he had info I was sure he would have told me by now.

I would just have to hang around Porter's office until I caught one of these guys going in to visit. I'd confront him then.

CHAPTER TWENTY-FIVE

Chloe loves apple pie too

Grant was walking out the diner's door. I hadn't noticed his truck when I'd pulled into the diner's parking lot. Hoping that he wouldn't notice me, I slid down in the seat. I peeked out the side window of my car and watched as he climbed into his truck. He started the engine and backed out.

When he'd pulled out onto the road, I straightened in the seat and released a sigh of relief. That had been a close one. I felt bad for hiding from him—he had been nothing but nice to me since I'd returned—but it was what I had to do. He didn't need to be involved with finding my uncle and I didn't need to be involved with Grant.

What had he been doing anyway? That was kind of a stupid question. It was a restaurant. Of course he'd come to eat. That was exactly what I would have told him I was doing there if he'd seen me. But in reality, I was coming to talk with Anna Louise. She didn't like Gina, but she seemed to be fine with me. Plus she'd dated my uncle, so that should make her want to help me. Since I had no other leads, I had to use the one that I could find. Even if it was probably pointless.

There were few cars in the parking lot, so I figured I would get a chance to talk with her. That was if she was actually working. I crossed my fingers, hoping that I would get lucky and she'd be there. I stepped inside the diner and looked around the mostly empty space. There were a few people in the back. They looked up at me when I entered, but then turned back to their food. I didn't see anyone who was actually working there. I decided against sitting at a booth. I'd just take a seat at the counter. Maybe someone would notice me soon.

If Anna Louise wasn't working, I'd ask if she would be in soon. That was probably information that they wouldn't give out to me though. I sat at the counter next to the register and grabbed a menu. I hadn't planned to eat, but she would probably be more likely to talk if I ordered something. The apple pie looked good. I perused the menu and kept glancing around to see if anyone was working. Noise sounded from in the kitchen, but whoever was back there hadn't noticed me yet. I placed the menu down and tapped my fingers against the counter.

I was just about to get up to see if I could find anyone when Anna Louise popped around the corner. She paused and looked at me as if she'd seen a ghost. That was never a good look to receive. Was she expecting to see me with Gina again? We'd made eye contact, so there was no way she could get out of coming over to help me. I wasn't sure what she was afraid of, it wasn't like I would bite her or anything.

I glanced over my shoulder to make sure that no one was standing behind me. Yes, it was definitely me she was looking at that way. Anna Louise grabbed a coffee pot and shuffled over. She turned the mug in front of me over and poured coffee without saying a word.

Finally, she said, "Looks as if I am popular today."

I quirked a brow. "Did you have a lot of customers?"

She shook her head. "No, I mean Mr. Grant Kenner was just in here to see me." Well, I had known that he'd just left, but I hadn't known he'd come in specifically to see her. That was interesting. "And now you are here."

"He was here to see you?"

She nodded. "Yes, ma'am. What can I get you?"

I eyed the apple pie and decided to give in and get a slice. "I'll take the apple pie."

She placed her hands on her hips and stared at me. "What?"

"Is it not good?"

She shook her head and turned around to retrieve the pie. I wasn't sure what that was all about.

"So what did he want?" I asked as she had her back toward me.

"He wanted to ask some questions," she said as she turned around and placed the plate in front of me. "No ice cream, right?"

I nodded. "Right. I like it without the ice cream."

"I figured as much." She smirked.

"What did he ask you?" I asked as I sank the fork into the flaky crust.

She poured me a glass of water and placed it in front of me.

"Thanks," I said.

"He wanted to ask about Porter Brennan. I guess that's why you're here too. Did he tell you to order the pie too?"

"No, he doesn't know I'm here."

She smiled. "That's even funnier."

This conversation was confusing me. I felt as if I was missing something that I should know. After taking a bite of the pie, I asked, "What did you tell Grant?"

Anna Louise released a deep breath. "What can I say? I told him nothing because I don't know anything. If you all want to know anything about Porter you should just go ask."

"I don't think it would be as easy as that."

"Why are you so interested in him anyway?" she asked.

"Because he seems to have a problem with me." I wouldn't mention the tape or possible blackmail.

"He has a problem with a lot of people," she said under her breath.

"Who else does he have a problem with?"

She shook her head. "Nothing."

Anna Louise walked over and helped another customer, but I wasn't going to give up just yet. I watched her and I knew she was aware of my stare. She tried to avoid looking at me.

Finally, she made eye contact and came back over. "Do you need something else?"

I needed something, but it wasn't food or drink. Maybe I needed to come up with another way to ask her about Porter. I could trick her into talking about him. Oh, who was I kidding? I had no plan to get her to open up to me.

"Why would he ask me to leave town?" I asked.

"Maybe it's because he didn't like you."

I shook my head. "Don't think so. He doesn't even know me. I just came back to town. I think he has something against my uncle. I think he doesn't like him and for that reason doesn't like me."

Her expression changed. I thought I was on to something.

"Why didn't he like my uncle? You would know that since you know both of them," I said.

"I don't know that. Whatever was going on between them is none of my business."

"So there *was* something between them."

"Are you ordering anything else?" she asked, trying to change the subject.

"You know, I won't stop until I find out. Did he do something to my uncle?" I asked.

She met my gaze. "I certainly hope not."

There was sincerity in her voice. Her answer hadn't made me feel better. Now I was worried that Porter had actually done something to my uncle. I placed cash for my pie on the counter and pushed to my feet.

"Thanks," I said.

I was thanking her for the pie and not the information because she'd provided me with little details to go on. Although now I was sure there had been something going on with Porter Brennan and my uncle. After all, I practically had the tape to prove it. I headed out of the diner with no clue what I was doing next. I needed to tell Grant about what Anna Louise had said. I had to tell someone and he was the first person who had popped into my head. Sure, I didn't want to involve him, but damn it, I couldn't keep myself away from him.

CHAPTER TWENTY-SIX

Grant would fight for Chloe in more ways than one

I was headed to my parents' store when I spotted one of the men who had been hanging around with Porter. It wasn't the one I thought had been at my office, but I wasn't going to let this one get away without saying something to him. He had been at the bar with Porter. If one of the inspector's sidekicks was around, then the other one couldn't be too far away.

The guy was across the street, so I needed to hurry before he had a chance to slip away. So far he hadn't noticed me. I waited for a couple cars to pass so that I could cross the street, but I didn't take my eyes off him.

When I crossed the street I ran after him. "Hey," I yelled out as I grew closer.

If he heard me, he didn't turn around. So I called out to him again. He finally glanced over his shoulder, but didn't stop. The man quickened his pace and I figured he would take off in a sprint at any moment. The last thing I needed was to have to chase this guy down the street. Before he had a chance to run, I kicked it into high gear. He was pretty slow-moving, so I figured I had a good chance of catching him.

When I was right behind him, I reached out to grab him. He yanked his shoulder away, so I reached out again.

This time I made good contact with his shoulder. "Hey, I'm talking to you. Why are you running away?"

He turned around and looked me in the eyes. "What the hell do you want?"

I didn't let my stare falter. "I want to talk with you. Didn't you hear me call to you?"

"I heard you, but I chose to ignore you. You got a problem with that?"

This guy had an attitude problem.

I shook my head. "No problem with you."

Without warning, the guy took a swing at me. I ducked and threw a punch at him. Unfortunately, it missed him too. It looked like we were both off this morning.

"You want to go with me?" he asked, while motioning for me to take another punch. People were beginning to stare at us now.

"I don't want to fight you. I just came to ask you a couple of questions. Why don't you make it easy on both of us and just answer a few questions," I said.

He looked around and then finally put his fists down to his sides. "What the hell do you want to know?"

"Tell me what you know about Porter Brennan."

He stared at me as if I wasn't speaking his language. I needed to explain more obviously.

"You're friends with him, right? You two seem to be together a lot. So I want to know what his problem is with the young woman the other night at the bar. And I want to know what was going on between Porter and her uncle." I figured my questions were pretty straight forward.

"I don't know what you are talking about," he said.

The guy shifted his gaze and I figured my window of opportunity to ask him any questions was limited before he took off again.

"Look, don't play games with me. I know you know him because I saw you with him. He had to have said something to you the other night when you were in the bar. What did he say about the woman at the bar?" I pushed.

"He said he thought she was hot."

That just made my blood boil. I was sick of their mind games and wanted to punch both of them. But I knew fighting with him wasn't going to get me anywhere, so I decided to try to calm down and be halfway nice to the guy. It wouldn't be easy though.

"I don't want to cause any trouble for you, but I just want to know what's going on. You can understand that, right? I'm sure you're a decent guy, so I would appreciate it if you could help me out by giving me the answers to my questions."

The guy didn't stop frowning, so I figured my attempt at being nice wasn't working either. I was out of ideas.

"Who are you anyway?" he asked with a scowl. "Why should I tell you anyway?"

"Why shouldn't you? I'm just asking a couple simple questions. My name's Grant Kenner, I'm the game warden. What's your name?"

He eyed me up and down and then said, "Charles Carr."

"Okay, Charles, what do you owe Porter?" I asked.

"I've got to go, it was nice chatting with you." He motioned over his shoulder.

I had to think of something fast. "Who's that other guy hanging out with Porter? Is he moving in on your business? Are you guys into some kind of crime?"

I made sure to give him a flash of my gun. His eyes traveled down to my waistband. That must have done the trick.

Charles released a deep breath. "Look, I just do what he tells me. I don't know what to tell you."

"Are you involved in crime with him? Is he doing something illegal?"

"I don't know what he's doing. Like I said, I just do what he tells me."

"What does that mean? You're following his orders? You do his dirty work for him? Did that dirty work have anything to do with getting rid of her uncle? Was Taylor in Porter's way?" I asked.

He stared at me blankly. They were pretty straightforward questions. It only needed a yes or no answer. "Man, you ask too many questions."

"I want to know why you follow his orders."

It was like I had to beat the answers out of him. Frankly, I was getting tired of standing there and getting no direct answers. I supposed I should just give up because I was getting nowhere. Although based on his reactions I knew they were involved in something illegal. Now I just needed to know what that something was before it was too late. I knew they would be after Chloe and that made me sick to my stomach.

"So when you were at the bar did he tell you to go up to Chloe and harass her?"

"Hey, I didn't do anything to your girlfriend. I'm sorry and you can tell her that I'm sorry."

I was sure Chloe would care about his apology. I didn't think he was being sincere, he just wanted to get away from me.

"I'll make sure to give her the message. You still didn't answer the question, did Porter tell you to go up to her?" I said.

"No," Charles snapped.

"So do you work for him then? Is that still your answer?"

"Yeah, I guess I work for him," Charles mumbled.

"What kind of work?" I asked.

He shrugged and pulled out a cigarette. "Whatever he needs me to do."

"So what did he have you do to her uncle?" I asked.

"I don't know what you mean. I didn't do anything to anyone. Porter just sometimes asks me to deliver things for him." Charles lit his cigarette.

"Like drugs? Or cash?"

He took a drag from the cigarette and then said, "I don't know. I don't look into the packages. It's none of my business."

"Don't you care if you're potentially delivering something illegal?" I asked.

"I guess I hadn't thought about it," he said. This guy wasn't the smartest one around.

"Why would you do something like that for him?" I asked.

Charles blew out smoke. "He helped me."

"He helped you do what?" I pushed.

"Just when I was in trouble, he helped me so now I help him."

"So he's blackmailing you too?" I asked.

"Man, you like to put words in my mouth."

I nodded. "You can tell him I was asking about him."

"I'm not telling him shit. I don't want him to know that I was talking about his business."

So Charles was afraid of Porter. It seemed a lot of people in town were afraid of him. Yeah, that was fine I would tell him myself. I needed to have a talk with that man anyway. I wasn't afraid of him.

"You were with Porter and the other man the other night on the boat. He tried to break into my office. What was he looking for?"

"Man, I guess he was looking for the girl. We watched her on the boat. He probably wanted to see if there was anything worth stealing while you were out there on the water. I have to go," he said, looking over his shoulder. "This conversation never happened, you hear?"

I held my hands up. "Whatever you say."

But it was too late. I knew that I was on to something. The guy turned around and walked away. I watched, but he didn't turn back around and look at me.

I had to decide what I was going to do from here. Talking with the inspector was my next step. I had to have some proof before going to my brother with this. It was unlikely I would get that from talking with Porter though.

As I turned around to head back to my parents' store, I felt someone watching me. I looked back over my shoulder to see if Charles was back there again, but he'd already turned the corner and was out of sight. People on the sidewalk had watched our fight, but they'd moved along after the action died down. Yet I knew someone was watching me. When I reached my parents' door, I stopped to look around again. There were quite a few cars parked against the curb, but they all looked unoccupied.

When I looked at the parking lot across the street that was when I spotted the face in the car looking back at me. It was the inspector. I immediately made eye contact with him. Just the sight of him made my blood boil. If he had something to say to me then he needed to face me like a man. After looking for traffic, I took off across the street. When I reached the parking lot, his car engine cranked. I darted behind another parked car just in case he decided he wanted to use his car as his weapon.

He revved the engine and then took off out of the parking lot. His tires squealed as he pulled out onto the street. I leaned against the car and stared out at the street. What the hell had just happened?

How long had Porter been watching me? I wondered if he'd watched my conversation with Charles. More than likely he had. People on the street were watching again. I spotted my mother at the door of her store standing there with her hands on her hips. She hadn't spotted me across the street yet. I was shocked that she had sensed me. She had that mother's intuition down pat.

Before I went back to the store I needed to call Ty. At least I had the name of this guy Charles Carr to give him. Maybe Ty could see what he could dig up on him. There were bound to be a few previous arrests on his record. After a couple rings Ty picked up.

"I have a name for you," I said.

"Let me have it."

After I filled him in on the conversation and Porter's reckless driving, Ty asked, "What are you doing now?"

"I'm headed over to Mom and Dad's. Don't tell them anything about this."

"Yeah, I won't say anything, but you know Mom has a way of finding out about this stuff."

"Well, keep it from her as long as possible," I warned.

"I'll see what I can find out and give you a call back," he said.

After hanging up, I headed across the street. My mother had gone back inside the store and people had forgotten about the disturbance.

"You just missed some jackass driving like a maniac," she said when I walked through the door.

I'd pretend that I hadn't caused that jackass to act the way that he had.

*

I'd left the store after helping my parents restock a couple shelves when Ty called.

"I've got a little bit of information for you," he said.

"Oh yeah, what's that?" I pulled over to the side of the road.

"This guy has been arrested before. Just misdemeanor stuff. Disorderly conduct. He's not from Belle Grove. He seems to be a real troublemaker though. It's probably only a matter of time before he does something worse," Ty said.

"That doesn't help explain why he would be in Belle Grove, but I appreciate that you looked into it."

"Not a problem. I'll keep an eye on him," Ty said.

CHAPTER TWENTY-SEVEN

Chloe feels helpless

I decided I needed to call Gina. I wasn't sure what she could help with, but it was better than going at this alone. After a few rings I was almost ready to hang up.

"Any news?" I asked when she picked up the phone.

"I'm not sure, but I need to talk with you. There's something I need to tell you," she said around a sigh.

"How about meeting me in twenty minutes?"

She agreed to meet me at the diner where I'd just been with Grant and I hung up the phone. There were other restaurants in Belle Grove and I'd hoped she would have suggested one, but this would give me a chance to speak with Anna Louise again.

I grabbed my purse and jumped in the car. Before I headed over for the diner I needed to pick up a few things. This was the same little drug store that I had shopped at as a teenager. When my parents needed anything they would send me here. I'd picked up my mother's medicine here before she died. It was impossible to escape memories in this town. Sometimes that was a good thing and sometimes it was very bad. This was one of the bad ones. After grabbing a few necessities, I made my way back to the diner parking lot.

Traffic was heavy around the diner and I wondered if they were having a special on their hamburgers. But when I neared, many police cars were in the diner's parking lot. What was going on? I pulled up to the curb down the way and headed back toward the diner. There was even police tape blocking off the parking lot. This didn't look good. Maybe there had been a robbery. There hadn't been a lot of crime in Belle Grove, but now I was beginning to wonder what was happening to this small town.

When I walked up to the parking lot entrance I realized that there was no way I was getting in there. The odd thing was that there was a lot of movement around Gina's car. My stomach twisted and for a moment I wondered if something had happened to her. I needed to stop thinking of such terrible scenarios. Everything would be fine. What could possibly have happened? There were some people standing nearby and I walked over to them.

"Do you know what happened?" I asked.

The woman looked at me with a sad expression. "Someone was murdered, but we don't know who yet."

Now my stomach really took a dive. Murdered? At the diner parking lot? In Belle Grove? This was crazy.

"Chloe." The man's voice came from behind me.

I knew who it was before I turned around. When I spun around Grant was behind me. His expression made my stomach turn.

"What's wrong?" I asked.

He shook his head. "It's Gina. She's been murdered."

It was as if someone had knocked me to the ground. "What happened?" I couldn't believe what he was telling me. "Are you sure?" I asked, hoping that he was wrong.

"Yes, I spoke with my brother. She was in her car." His voice was somber.

"Someone murdered her in her car? In the parking lot?" I asked, still in a daze.

He frowned. "Yes, she was still in her car."

I shook my head. "I was supposed to meet her here." I knew it wasn't my fault, but maybe if I hadn't asked her to meet me this wouldn't have happened. "I shouldn't have asked her to meet me," I whispered.

He shook his head. "Don't even say that."

I looked out over the parking lot, still stunned by what he'd told me. When was the last time anyone had been murdered in Belle Grove?

"Who would do this to her?" I asked.

I didn't expect that he'd have an answer, but I had to ask.

"It was a waitress who worked at the diner. She wasn't working this morning when we were there."

I stared at him for a moment. "Do you know the name?" I asked.

He shook his head. "Her name is Anna Louise."

My eyes widened. "She dated the inspector. She and Gina didn't like each other."

"What makes you say that?" he asked.

"Gina told me when we ate here together." Apparently, Gina had been right when she said she didn't like her.

"The waitress says it was self-defense," Grant said.

My mouth dropped. "You can't be serious. I didn't know Gina well, but I can't imagine she would have ever done anything to that woman. Anna Louise was hostile toward Gina the day we saw her."

"Do you know why they didn't like each other?" he asked

"I guess they had words before."

"I'm sure that's something the police will be able to find out," he said.

"I hope they get to the bottom of this soon," I said. What would my uncle do when he found out? I had to find him and let him know. "I just don't believe that Anna Louise would have killed her in self-defense."

He shoved his hands into his pockets. "It is hard to believe. Gina was so quiet and she seemed easy-going."

"Where is the waitress now?" I asked.

He motioned with a tilt of his head. "They arrested her already."

I stared across the parking lot. "Is Gina still there?"

He looked down for a moment and then nodded. "Yes."

I couldn't believe what had happened. This had totally changed everything.

Grant looked at me and said, "Are you sure you're okay?"

I nodded. "Yes, I'll be fine. Gina wanted to tell me something." I stared out at the parking lot. "That was why we were meeting here."

Grant touched my arm and spun me around to face him. "Hey, you didn't know this was going to happen."

I nodded. "But what did she want to tell me? I'll never know now. Did it have something to do with my uncle?" I frowned.

"We'll find him."

I wanted to believe him, but with each passing day it seemed more and more unlikely. I had wanted to know why Grant wanted to help me, but right now, I didn't care. I was just glad he wanted to.

I had to find out what Gina had wanted to tell me. It couldn't be a coincidence that she was murdered right before telling me something. There had to be something with the fact that she had something to tell me and then she was dead. Would anyone know what Gina had wanted to tell me or had she kept it a secret? I realized that I knew less about Gina than I'd thought I did. I didn't even know if she had any family. Maybe she had friends she had confided in. Someone had to know something.

What did I know about this waitress? Not a lot of anything. But I would try to find out all that I could. There was one thing I knew about her and that was that she'd dated the inspector. Maybe I needed to pay him a little visit. Grant wouldn't like that, but he didn't even have to know. It would be my secret. Sure, Porter gave me the creeps, but I had no other option. I couldn't just sit back and do nothing. What kind of niece would I be if I didn't keep trying to find my uncle?

And now I had to find out about his girlfriend. There had to be a connection between the inspector and the waitress. And he probably knew why she had killed Gina.

This was becoming more of a tangled web with each passing minute. I would go visit Porter Brennan as soon as I got away from here. Plus, I wanted to leave before they took Gina away. I just couldn't stand to see that.

The crowd had grown even larger now. This would be a lot of gossip for Belle Grove. It would be the talk all over town and rightfully so.

"Are you okay?" Grant asked, breaking me out of my thoughts.

I glanced over at him. "Yes, I'm okay."

"You looked like you zoned out there for a while," he said.

"I guess I just have a lot to think about."

"What are you doing now?" he asked.

"I have a few things I need to do," I said. I hoped he couldn't figure out what I was up to.

"You know the police might want to talk with you since you were meeting her here."

I nodded. "Yeah, that's okay. They know where to find me."

He touched my arm again. "Is it okay if I walk you to your car?"

I knew I should have said no, but I found myself nodding instead. "Sure."

We started off down the sidewalk and walked in silence. What was there to say? This was a strange moment.

"So you're not going to tell me where you're headed now?" he asked.

I shook my head. "I just have some things to do."

"You're not going to get yourself into trouble, are you?"

I stopped beside my car. "What makes you say that?"

His gaze ran up and down my body. "It's just a feeling."

"Of course not," I said, trying a little smile.

I opened the car door and didn't give him a chance to kiss me this time. Although I wanted his lips on mine. I could tell myself that I didn't, but it would be a lie. Why was I fighting it?

Now that Gina was gone I felt completely lost. I didn't know which way to turn. I had to pull myself together. This was no time to fall apart. As I looked in my rear-view mirror, I watched Grant walk away. I wondered if he felt my eyes on him. Part of me wanted to call out to him and ask him to come with me.

Porter Brennan's office was in front of me. I stared up at the two-story building. When I'd looked up the information, it said the inspector's office was on the first floor. Wouldn't he be surprised to see me? Confronting him was a crazy idea and I knew that, but it was something I felt I had to do. Would he be able to look me in the eyes and tell me he didn't have anything to do with the fact that my uncle had vanished. I would step right into his office and demand an answer.

Swallowing the lump in my throat, I pushed forward and through the main door of the old brick building. A hallway stretched out in front of me and another hallway on the left. There was a closed door on the right marked do not enter. I figured the names would be listed on the doors, so finding his office would be easy. My heart pulsed quickly as I walked down the hallway in front of me. Looking from side to side, I checked each door. Some had names and others didn't. When I reached the end of the hallway, I still hadn't located his office.

Turning around, I hurried back down the hallway and turned to my right. I hoped that I hadn't read the wrong address. I wouldn't give up hope just yet, not until I'd checked every door down the other hallway. Again I looked at each door as I made my way down. When I'd almost reached the end, I spotted the building inspector words on the door. My stomach flipped. Now I really would have to confront him. I'd never been good with confrontation, but sometimes you had to do things you didn't enjoy. Now I had to hope that Porter was actually in there.

I positioned my fist next to the door, ready to knock. Before I actually did it, I stopped. I was having second thoughts. After the way Porter had acted at the bar, he didn't seem like the friendliest guy in town. Now I was going right into his spider web. But I could handle myself, right? If he was a jerk, I would just leave. Actually, I knew he would be a jerk, but how big of a jerk was the question. Not wasting another minute, I pounded on the door.

"Yeah," he said in a clipped town.

That must have been my signal that it was okay to enter. I hadn't expected for Porter to be any friendlier than that. When I pushed the door open, he looked up from his paperwork.

His eyes narrowed when he spotted me. "What are you doing here?"

Was that any way to greet someone? My uneasiness grew instantly.

"I came to ask you some questions about my uncle Taylor Beaumont." I figured there was no sense in beating around the bush. I'd just get right to the point. The more he glared at me though, the more I was reconsidering my decision to come to his office.

"I doubt that I can help you any," he said, looking down at his paperwork.

I stepped closer to his desk until I was finally standing right in front of it. I crossed my arms in front of my chest and stared at him. He still hadn't bothered to glance up at me again. He was trying to pretend that I was insignificant, but I wouldn't allow him to intimidate me with that game.

"I think you can help me."

That comment still didn't make him pay any attention to me. He was such an arrogant jerk.

"What I want to know is if you have any idea where my uncle is," I said matter-of-factly.

"Why in the hell would I know where he is?" His stare was now fixed on me.

Porter's anger had increased in a split second. I sensed that he didn't like my topic of discussion.

"Do my questions make you uncomfortable?" I asked.

Waves of rage shot off of him. "Nothing makes me uncomfortable," he snapped.

Sweat was breaking out on my forehead, but I wouldn't let him stop me. I didn't take my eyes off him. Of course he didn't stop staring at me either.

Porter shoved the paperwork to the side and pushed to his feet. His stare followed me as he slowly made his way around his desk.

I swallowed hard and said, "Don't think that you can intimidate me because it won't work."

My words probably didn't sound all that confident. But I'd given it my best shot. Within a second, Porter was standing in front of me. I stepped back, putting more distance between us. He just moved forward though, closing the gap. I had to stand my ground in spite of the fact that he looked like he wanted to punch me in the face.

I didn't doubt for two seconds that he wouldn't hit a woman. Now that I thought about it more, it was probably best if I didn't stand my ground and if I just got the heck out of there. Before I had a chance to turn around and leave, Porter reached out and shoved me. I stumbled backward, unable to right myself. I fell onto the leather chair behind me. Now Porter stood over me, hovering like a spider ready to pounce on a fly. I'd been right; I had walked right into his spider web.

I placed my hands on his chest and shoved, but he pushed me back onto the chair. Porter leaned down, placing his hands on my arms. His grip was like a vise. He had me pinned down and I didn't know how I would get out of this situation. Porter had more strength that me. The only advantage I had right now was that I could probably get my knee positioned right between his legs. One good kick would bring him to his knees.

CHAPTER TWENTY-EIGHT

Grant didn't want to lose Chloe again

After a few steps, I turned around to watch Chloe drive away. I hated seeing her so upset and it was even worse knowing that there was nothing I could do to help her. All I could do was keep trying to find her uncle. If in fact he'd left on his own, then he had no idea how this had affected her. With each passing day the chances of something bad happening to him increased. Eventually he would have to show up or leave a trace. The odds were in our favor, at least I hoped they were in our favor.

A strange feeling poked at me as if I was missing something. That feeling also told me that Chloe was up to something. Would she get herself into trouble? I hoped not. I couldn't stand the thought of something bad happening to her. I wouldn't let that happen. Not as long as she was in Belle Grove. If she was near me then I would do my best to protect her. This situation had just turned deadly and I didn't want Chloe to meet the same fate as Gina. Chloe might be in over her head with this one. Hell, I might be in over my head too.

I turned around and walked back to talk with my brother. The crowd had already thinned out. It looked cut-and-dry, but maybe something new had turned up. It was suspicious that this had happened to Gina right when the uncle had disappeared. I wouldn't be surprised if there was a connection. But how in the hell would I find that connection? No one ever wanted to talk around here. Although as much as they wanted to keep secrets, the secrets always came out in the end. It was human nature to talk and share stories.

My brother spotted me and walked over. "Hey, what's going on?" he asked.

I shoved my hands in my pockets and looked around. "Not much. Anything new?"

He shook his head. "No, not yet."

"Listen, I thought I'd tell you first that the reason Gina was here was to meet Chloe. I doubt it means anything, but I just thought I'd let you know."

He looked at me for a moment, but didn't make any wise comments about Chloe. "Why were they meeting? Just for lunch? It sounds like there's more to the story."

I nodded. "There's a little more to the story, yes. Chloe said that Gina had something she wanted to tell her. Of course Chloe didn't have a chance to find out because Gina was killed."

He nodded and cast a sideways glance at me. "Now that is more to the story. I'll look into it. We're questioning the waitress now. If she knows anything we should find out. Thanks for letting me know." He patted me on the back.

I smiled. "Yeah, you'll let me know what you find out."

He nodded. I watched as he joined the other officers, then turned around toward my truck. It was time for me to get out of there.

I headed out of town toward my office. I wasn't sure what I would do there. But it would give me a chance to clear my thoughts. It was typical of me though. Going in to work on my day off. I really had no other life other than my work. That needed to change. But how would I change that? It was something I would have to figure out. Of course visions of Chloe's sweet face popped into my head when I thought of making that change. I wondered what she would say about that. She probably wouldn't like it much.

No one was in the office right now. I plopped down at my desk and looked at a few papers. I shoved them out of the way and leaned my head back against my chair and closed my eyes. It didn't help though because I couldn't stop thinking of Chloe and wondering what she was doing or if she was in danger. Being here was doing nothing and was getting me nowhere. There was only one thing I could do to change the current situation, I had to go find her. I jumped up from my desk and back to my truck.

I retraced my path and made it back into town. When I passed the diner again most of all the police cars were gone. I couldn't imagine how stunned the diners must have been when they witnessed Gina being killed. What if Chloe had been there when it happened? She might have been shot too. I didn't even want to think about it.

I wasn't sure where to even look for Chloe. I didn't know what was going on in her head. I turned into the hotel parking lot, but after circling around the whole space I didn't see her car. I turned down a few streets aimlessly. I was beginning to think that this was a pointless trip. I was thinking about giving up when I spotted a car that looked exactly like Chloe's. I wasn't sure, so I circled the block and pulled up behind the car. When I walked over to the window and looked in, I wasn't sure it was her car. The part that was most upsetting was if this was her, she was parked in front of the inspector's building. I prayed that she hadn't gone in there to talk with him.

I made it around the car and up the steps of the building. Wouldn't he be surprised to see me again so soon. There was no one around, so I made my way down the hall toward his office. My stomach turned just thinking about Chloe confronting this guy. After the way he'd acted at the bar I didn't want her anywhere around him. This jerk needed to be put in his place and I was ready to do it.

I marched toward his door on a mission. The door was closed and my stomach did a flip.

I really started to freak out when I heard Chloe's voice from the other side of the door. She had come here after all. I turned the knob, but the door was locked. The creep had her in there with the door locked. She was telling him to get off of her, so I knew this was a life-or-death situation. Thank goodness I had shown up.

I didn't bother knocking because I knew he wouldn't answer the door. But that left me little choice on what I could do. I had only one option as far as I could tell.

I moved back away from the door and then ran full force at it. The door broke open in a clean cut. Chloe was sitting at the chair with the inspector with his hands on her. She was attempting to push him away. And based on the position of her leg I thought she was ready to give him a hit to the groin. I closed the distance between us in two steps. His eyes widened when he looked up and saw me coming toward him. I was going to pound him into the ground.

I pulled my fist back and slammed it into the inspector's jaw. He stumbled back, holding his face. Chloe jumped up and ran for the door. I grabbed him by his shirt and yanked him to his feet. He stared at me with wide eyes.

"I don't want to ever see you touching her again. Do you understand?"

He nodded, but didn't speak. I shoved him and he fell to the floor again. He was lucky I didn't hit him again. I stared at him for a moment longer and then turned for the door. Chloe had already walked out.

When I reached the hallway, I spotted Chloe. I raced after her. When I called out she didn't turn around. Finally, I reached her and grabbed her arm. She reached her arm back and smacked me. I groaned and held my face.

Her hand flew to her mouth. "I'm so sorry. I didn't know it was you."

"That's okay. You've got quite a punch."

She shrugged. "He had me cornered back there or I would have punched him."

"No need to worry about him, I don't think he'll bother you again," I said.

"What did you do to him?" she asked.

"I just told him the way that it was going to be. How I expect him to treat you from now on."

She nodded.

"Why did you go there?" I asked.

She shook her head.

I crossed my arms in front of my chest. "Come on, why don't you tell me?"

"I just feel like he knows about my uncle. I wanted to know why he told me to get out of here," she said.

"What did he say to you?" I asked.

"He told me to mind my own business. That was the extent of the conversation before he decided to turn violent."

I touched her arm and a shiver went down my spine. "Come on, let me drive you back to your hotel. You don't need to drive right now. You're too stressed. I'll bring you back to your car later."

She stared for a beat and then nodded. "Okay."

I hoped she didn't think I had suggested taking her back there because I expected anything to happen between us. Nevertheless, she had agreed and that was all that mattered at the moment. We walked to my truck and I held the door open for her.

"Thanks," she said softly. She leaned her head against the truck's seat and released a deep breath. "I can't believe that guy. Has he always been that way?"

I turned onto the side street. "He has been an ass since he got to town."

"Why does he still have a job here?" she asked.

"That's a good question," I said.

We pulled into the hotel parking lot and I shoved the truck into park. She stared straight ahead for a moment.

"I can come back and get you when you need your car," I offered.

She looked at me. "Would you like to come in?"

Maybe I sounded crazy, but I was almost ready to say no. I didn't want her to think that I was just trying to get a kiss from her. Not that she was inviting me in for that reason. Hell, this whole thing was too damn confusing.

Finally, I shut off the ignition. "Yes, I'd like that." What could I say? After all, I was a man and I wasn't going to turn down her invitation.

"I just need to take a shower and then you can take me back to my car. I need to wash off the awful feeling he left on me."

I followed her into the room. In spite of the sun outside the room was dim.

She set her purse on the table. "I'm just going to take a shower." She motioned over her shoulder. "You can watch TV or something if you'd like."

I smiled. "Thanks."

She disappeared into the bathroom and I tried to distract myself with the TV. Flashes of her body ran through my mind. The water running didn't help to stop the thoughts either. I imagined the water running over every curve of her body. I shook off the thought. I needed to take a cold shower. I had to stop thinking about Chloe, but that was virtually impossible.

After a couple more minutes Chloe appeared from the bathroom. She was wearing a pink fuzzy robe and her hair was wet. She looked just as beautiful as ever.

She smiled and shrugged. "You like the bunnies?" She pointed at the white rabbits on her robe.

"Cute," I said with a smile.

She sat on the edge of the bed and I moved closer to her.

"What are you thinking?" she asked.

I touched her hand. "About how beautiful you are and what a fool I am for letting you go."

I leaned close and pressed my lips against hers.

CHAPTER TWENTY-NINE

Chloe wonders why she wasted all this time

I couldn't believe that his lips were on mine again. He moved his mouth over mine with ease and it was as if this was where I belonged all along. I had missed out on this for the past ten years. He was definitely making up for that lost time now.

Grant ran his hands through my hair as his tongue traveled along with mine. I'd never had a kiss like this before. Grant nibbled on my bottom lip. I felt him smile and then he brushed his full lips over mine again. I couldn't have stopped for a million dollars.

As his mouth moved across mine, his hands traced along my arms, and then he caressed my face. His hands gently caressed the exposed parts of my skin, all the while moving his lips down to my neck and back up to my lips. I released a soft moan and he kissed me hard again. He leaned his head back and stared into my eyes, then pressed his mouth against mine again. His lips were soft and warm and I hoped he wouldn't stop. Grant pulled me closer and pressed his hard chest against my breasts. His body felt so good next to mine and all I wanted was to feel him naked.

As he pulled me closer, we moved back onto the bed. I tossed the cover out of the way and Grant moved his body on top of mine. His hands were in my hair as he moved his lips on my neck and then down to my cleavage. His luscious lips wandered over my body, licking, sucking and teasing. My hands roamed over his chest and down to his hard stomach. Grant's low groan of approval vibrated through my body. What would it feel like to touch his bare skin? I wanted to find out and I wanted to rip his shirt off right then. Grant's hands had found their way to my breasts. He lightly caressed them through my robe.

Grant watched me, gauging my reaction. I gave him the silent signal that we should remove the clothing right away. He slowly untied my robe and released a deep breath when he looked at my exposed skin. Our eyes were locked on each other. I tugged at his shirt and he pulled it the rest of the way over his head. I unbuttoned his jeans and he pulled them the rest of the way off. Grant was fully aroused. He tossed the jeans on the floor and came back to bed, lying on top of me again. We kissed again with our bodies intertwined.

The feel of his naked body against mine sent me into overdrive. I'd forgotten about all the reasons I didn't want this to happen. His hands traveled across my body and I closed my eyes and enjoyed the feel of his hands. We didn't speak, but no words were needed. I wanted him and I knew that he wanted me too. Our bodies fit together and we moved in motion.

The time slipped away as we enjoyed each other's bodies. Grant held me in his arms and we drifted off to sleep.

*

I woke when a sliver of light splashed through a crack in the curtain. My mind was foggy, but when I looked over at the other side of the bed, I realized that it hadn't been a dream. The old feelings kept trying to come back, but I'd loved every minute that we had shared last night and I wanted to finally push the past away for good. The emotions of what had happened over the past few days overwhelmed me and I'd found comfort in Grant's arms.

Maybe Grant and I really could have a fresh start. Last night could have been just the beginning for us. Would he feel the same way? By the smile on his face I could tell the answer was yes.

"Good morning," he said as he touched my cheek. "How are you?"

I smiled. I was giddy, but I couldn't admit that to him. "I'm good," I offered instead.

He leaned up in bed. "What time is it?"

"It's eight," I said.

"I'm late for work and I still need to go home, shower, and get my uniform."

I frowned and he touched my face again.

"I wish you didn't have to go."

"I'll see you tonight after work?" he asked.

I smiled and nodded. "I'd like that."

I couldn't keep myself from smiling. He climbed out of bed and retrieved his clothing. I couldn't take my eyes off his muscular body.

"I should take you to your car," he said as he touched my arm.

I grabbed my robe and hurried into it. "Just let me get dressed," I said as I hopped up.

He pulled me close to him and kissed me again. I pushed him away. "You're going to be late."

He groaned playfully as I grabbed my clothing and headed for the bathroom. After a couple minutes, we were in his truck and headed toward my car.

"Last night was the most amazing night of my life," he said.

I couldn't stop smiling.

He pulled behind my car and jumped out when I opened my door. He rushed over and helped me out of the truck.

"I had a great time," I said.

He touched my face. "I'll call you soon so we can make plans for tonight."

I wanted to see him, but I hoped he hadn't forgotten that I was still on a mission to find my uncle. I nodded. "Have a great day."

"I will as long as I'm thinking of you," he said.

I waved and then climbed behind the wheel of my car. I tried not to look over at the inspector's building. I had to decide what to do from here. Things had definitely changed between Grant and me. What would I do? As wonderful as it had been last night, I couldn't change the fact that I lived in Arizona now. I wondered if Grant would leave Belle Grove? No way. His life was the bayou and last time I checked there were no bayous in Arizona. I couldn't just move because of one night, but the thought of not seeing Grant again made me sick to my stomach. I tried to push the thought out of my mind and just enjoy my time with him right now.

I drove back to the hotel and when I walked in all I could think about was Grant's body in my bed. Maybe if I grabbed breakfast I could shake the thought. There was no way I could go back to the diner after what had happened to Gina, but for all I knew the place wasn't even open today.

I jumped in the shower and then dressed. When I stepped over to the window, I noticed Grant's wallet on the table. He'd forgotten it. I supposed he would need it today which meant that I'd have to take it to him.

I grabbed my purse and keys and headed toward his office. I still couldn't wrap my mind around what had happened. Maybe he'd left the wallet there so I'd have an excuse to come and see him while he was at work. That was fine with me, although I needed to spend the day trying to find my uncle. I'd give Grant the wallet and then hurry out of there. We would see each other tonight. My stomach did a little dance just thinking about it. When I glanced in the mirror, I saw the silly smile on my face, but couldn't make it stop.

I reached the parking lot and pulled in. I spotted Grant's truck, so I pulled into the spot next to him. I shoved the car into park and then headed around the car toward his office. I walked up the path. When I glanced over I spotted my uncle's boat was in the same spot as when I'd taken it out on the water. I hadn't been back here since that night when we'd seen the man at Grant's door. It seemed that we would never find out who that was, or who the men had been on the boat. I knew one of them looked a lot like the inspector, but it had been far away so I wasn't sure.

I focused my attention on his office again, but I stopped in my tracks when I saw him. Grant wasn't alone. He was talking with a woman. Her back was facing me and Grant hadn't noticed me. There wasn't anything odd about that until he reached out and hugged her.

That wasn't what I'd wanted to see. Who was this woman? The embrace was more than I could handle, so I turned around and hurried away. I didn't want him to know that I'd been there. When I reached his truck, I tossed his wallet into the open window.

Now we had no reason to see each other again. What had I been thinking by allowing myself to get wrapped up with Grant Kenner again? I truly was a fool for falling for him again. It was still the same and nothing had changed. I should have known better, but I was too stupid to see. One trip back to Belle Grove and I'd fallen into his trap again. I hoped he didn't hear my car as I turned the key. What did he care if I was here anyway? The sooner I got out of there the better off I'd be.

I pulled the car out and took off for the street. When I glanced in the rear-view mirror, I noticed Grant running toward my car. There was a car driving by, so I couldn't pull out right away. I hoped that I could pull out before he reached my car. He was calling out to me, but I didn't want to talk to him. Finally, the car drove past and I pulled out onto the street in a hurry. When I glanced back, Grant had stopped running. He threw his hands up in the air, and then I drove out of sight.

I headed back to my room to pack. Maybe it was the wrong thing to do since I hadn't found my uncle, but I didn't know what else to do at this point. The police wouldn't report him missing and now Gina was dead. There was nothing else left for me in Belle Grove. I would try to find him from my house in Arizona. I shoved my belongings into my bags and headed out to my car. I shoved the bags in the trunk and then looked around the room one last time to see if I'd missed anything.

Flashes of the night before went through my mind. I cursed under my breath. A curl of anger whirled in my gut. A crimson haze surrounded my vision, but at the same time, tears burned the back of my throat. They were tears of sadness and disappointment, not from anger. The anger I felt was mostly frustration at myself for falling for Grant's act. Just then my cell phone rang. I looked at the number and saw that it was Grant. There was no way I was going to answer his call. I had to get out of there because he might come to my room soon. What did he care if I left anyway? He needed to leave me alone for good. There was nothing left for us to say to each other.

I closed the door behind me and headed to the office to turn in my key. Disappointment rushed through me that I couldn't help my uncle. I had let him down. I'd come to Belle Grove to find him, not get involved with the likes of Grant Kenner. When I stepped into the office the woman was behind the desk. She smiled as if she had a secret.

"Is everything okay?" she asked.

I nodded. "I'm checking out now."

Her eyebrow shot up. "So soon?"

I nodded, but didn't offer an explanation. She could ask Grant the reason behind my sudden departure.

After handing over the key, I got out of there before she had a chance to ask any more questions. As I walked back to my car, my cell rang again. I felt like tossing the phone into the nearest trash can. Why did he even bother calling when he should have known that I wouldn't answer? I groaned as I looked down at it again. That was when I realized that it wasn't Grant's number this time.

I recognized the number right away. It was my uncle.

My hand shook as I answered the call.

"Is it you?" I asked.

CHAPTER THIRTY

Grant doesn't want history to repeat itself

I spotted Chloe as she was running away. What was she doing there? That was when it hit me that she'd seen me hugging my cousin's wife. Stacy's mother was ill and in the hospital. Since my cousin was out of town, she'd come to tell me she would be visiting her mother. Now Chloe must have thought that I was with another woman, just like she'd thought before. It was history repeating itself. I could see why she would think that though. I'd never get her to talk with me again now, not after last night. She probably thought I'd deceived her on purpose.

Stacy ran up behind me. "Is everything okay?"

I ran my hand through my hair and released a deep breath. "Everything will be fine."

I didn't want to worry Stacy with my problems right now. She had a lot to deal with. She would blame herself and I didn't want that. This was all my fault. If I hadn't been stupid years ago then this wouldn't be a problem now. It was difficult to right mistakes that had been made. But I had to try, even if it would be my last chance.

"Who was that?" Stacy asked.

I glanced over at her since she was now standing beside me. I didn't say anything.

"Someone you're dating?" she asked. I nodded. "Well, I think she is upset with you."

I ran my hand through my hair. "Yes, I think she is slightly upset. I upset her a long time ago."

"Why haven't you mentioned her before?"

"It was a long time ago. She just recently came back to town." I was still trying to process what had happened in my mind. "We kind of were together last night," I said.

Stacy glared at me. Her eyes widened. "You kind of were together last night? What is wrong with you?" She smacked my arm. "Go after her." She motioned with her hands.

"If I know her, and I think I do, I doubt she wants me to go after her."

"Well, if you don't go after her you will regret it."

"I went after her years ago and she didn't respond to that well, I hardly think anything has changed now."

"You won't know unless you try," Stacy said.

I stared for a moment, and then nodded. "Okay."

She smiled. "Now that's more like it."

"Maybe I should try to call her first," I said.

She shrugged. "It couldn't hurt, but you should still go talk to her in person."

"Oh, I definitely will, but maybe if she'll talk to me on the phone first it will help." I touched my pants pocket and found my phone.

That was when I realized I didn't have my wallet. I must have left it in Chloe's room. She would probably toss it in the trash. I dialed her number and let it ring, but just as I suspected, she didn't answer.

"No answer," I said to Stacy.

She motioned. "Go to her. I need to leave anyway."

She hugged me and then went over to her car. I jumped in my truck and that was when I noticed my wallet on the seat. Chloe must have dropped it in there on her way out. At least she hadn't tossed it in the water. That was why she'd come to see me. I wanted to explain this mess more than anything, but my fear was that I wouldn't even get the chance. I pulled out of the parking lot and onto the street. I drove as fast as I could without risking my brother pulling me over and giving me a ticket.

After driving too fast though town, I pulled up to the hotel. As I was turning in, Chloe was pulling out. Our eyes met and she frowned. That was not the look that I had hoped for, but at least she hadn't flipped her middle finger. I pulled around in the lot and pointed the truck in the right direction to follow her. It was probably a useless maneuver though because it wasn't like she would stop for me. Heck, knowing Chloe she'd call the cops on me. She'd tell them that I was following her.

I pulled out onto the street and drove behind her. There was another car in front of me, but so far I was able to keep up. It looked as if she was headed out of town. She was probably driving back to Baton Rouge to the airport. My stomach sank when I realized that she was going back to Arizona. She'd never return to Belle Grove. I guessed she'd given up on finding her uncle. I couldn't blame her for wanting to leave and I probably shouldn't follow her all the way to the airport, but I would.

The more I drove, the more I realized that the car in front of me wasn't acting right. It was following way too close to Chloe's car. When I looked closer, I realized it was the inspector's car. He was following Chloe too, but I knew his motives weren't good like mine. The faster she drove the more he pursued her. I wanted to call her and tell her to stop, that I would take care of him, but I didn't want her to wreck by answering her phone. When I got my hands on this bastard I'd knock him out.

Chloe sped up, but then her car swerved. The car behind her had nudged hers. The next thing I knew, she was going off the road and into a ditch. The inspector's car didn't stop. Everything seemed in slow motion. The crunch of the metal as she slammed into the ditch. The screaming tires as she skidded off the road. She spun out, slamming into the ditch, and then the glass on her windshield shattered. For a moment, it felt as if my heart stopped beating.

Chloe hadn't gotten out of the car and I prayed that she would be okay. I couldn't handle it if something happened to her. I thought the inspector had noticed that I was behind him at that point. He could run now, but I would catch up with him later.

I wheeled my truck onto the road's shoulder and shoved it into park. I jumped out of the truck and ran toward the car.

"Chloe," I yelled out, but she didn't answer.

She still hadn't gotten out of the car. Panic had definitely set in now and I was fearing the worst. When I reached the car, I yanked the door open. Chloe had her hands on her head. The airbag had been deployed and the front of the car was smashed. She turned to look at me with a frightened look on her face. I reached in and pulled her out of the car.

"Are you okay?" I asked.

"I'm okay," she said as she attempted to steady her feet. She looked back at the car. "I smashed it up bad, huh?"

"Yes, it's done."

"That was the inspector," she said. "He bumped my car."

"I saw him. Come on, get in my truck. We're going after him."

She stared at me for a moment, then nodded. "Okay, I guess you have no other options at the moment."

I took her hand. "No, you don't. Thank goodness you're okay."

I didn't want her to wreck, but this would give me a chance to explain what had happened. Now if she would only give me that chance. I opened the car door and she hopped in.

"Are you sure you're okay?" I asked again.

She tucked her hair behind her ear and released a deep breath. "I'm fine."

I ran around to the other side and jumped behind the wheel. I cranked the engine and pulled back out onto the road. We probably wouldn't be able to catch up to him, but I would find him. I would hunt him down wherever he went. I wouldn't let him get away with this—not a chance.

I punched the gas and headed in the direction that I thought he'd gone. If I didn't see him I'd turn back and go to town. I'd go to his house if I had to.

"Do you have any idea why he was following you?" I asked.

She shook her head. "I don't know for sure. My guess is it has something to do with my uncle's disappearance. By the way, I have something to tell you," she said.

I glanced over at her as I drove. "Oh yeah, what's that? Should I be worried? Is something else wrong?"

"My uncle called just a few minutes ago."

I almost ran off the road. "Are you sure it was him?"

She nodded with a smile. "Oh yeah, I'm positive."

"Where in the hell is he?"

"He called to warn me. He'd heard about Gina and knew that I'd come to look for him. He took off because someone was threatening to kill him and his family."

"And he just now told you this? Who was threatening him?"

"My phone cut off and I didn't get a chance to find out."

I pulled my phone out. "Well, call him back with my phone."

I shoved the phone in her direction. Before she had a chance to take the phone I looked back to the road and noticed the inspector's car up ahead.

"We caught him," I said.

Just then the inspector's car swerved and he ran off the road. He crashed into the ditch almost exactly as Chloe had done miles back. But this time no one had forced him off the road—well, maybe karma had forced him off. I pushed the gas so that I could catch up before he had a chance to get out of the car.

I reached his car and pulled up behind him. I shoved the truck into park and hopped out. Chloe ran up behind me. The car door opened and he was trying to get out. I didn't bother to ask him if he was okay, because I honestly didn't care. He was getting what he deserved. He looked over at me and Chloe and his eyes widened. He probably knew that he had really pissed me off now. If he wasn't injured from the wreck then I was ready to do it on my own. He didn't speak as he moved away from the car.

When he reached the front of the car he ran. I didn't know where he thought he was going because I would catch him. I took off after him. He jumped across the ditch and into the line of trees. That would make it harder to find him, but I wouldn't give up. I jumped across the ditch and into the line of trees. The sun was blocked by the leaves and made it a little harder to see. I looked around, trying to see which direction he'd gone. That was when I saw him to my right running around the trees up ahead.

I was faster than him. I took off in a sprint after him. He glanced back and saw me. When he turned around, he tumbled to his knees. Before he had a chance to get on his feet again, I had reached him. He looked up as I stepped closer to him. He lifted his arms up as if that would block me from seeing him.

"Get up," I yelled.

"I didn't do anything wrong," he said.

"That's where you're wrong." I grabbed his shirt and yanked him to his feet.

He turned to face me and then pulled his arm back and swung it in my direction. I was able to duck just in time before his fist met my face. I straightened again and then swung a punch in his direction. Luckily, it made contact with his face and he went down to the ground. He grabbed his face and groaned.

"Having a bad day?" I asked. "Well, it's about to get worse."

"Why did you do with Taylor Beaumont?" I demanded.

A frown snapped between his brows. "I told him to get out of town. He was meddling into things that wasn't his business."

"Like you blackmailing people? Were you taking money in exchange for building permits? Gina and Taylor were on to you, weren't they? That's why you had to get rid of them?"

"I don't have to answer any of your questions." His jaw tightened as he glared at me.

"I think you'll feel differently when you're behind bars."

He looked at me and held his arm out. "Fine. I'll tell you everything."

I stared at him. "I'm listening. What do you want to tell me?"

CHAPTER THIRTY-ONE

Chloe is glad Grant came after her.

After Grant ran after Porter Brennan, I pulled out my phone. That was when I remembered that it wasn't working. I didn't know what I was going to do. I glanced over and saw Grant's phone on the seat next to me. I picked it up and pushed 911. I gave the woman our location and she promised that police were on their way. I wondered if Grant's brother would show up. What was I going to do in the meantime? I had to see if Grant needed my help. Had he found the inspector?

I had no other choice but to run toward the line of trees where Grant had just disappeared. What I would do if I found the men, I wasn't sure. Adrenaline surged through me, pushing me to find Grant and Porter. Anger poured through me, boiling my blood. Porter had tried to kill me when he ran me off the road.

When I reached the tree line, I paused and contemplated which way I should go. I hadn't watched to see which way Grant had gone. Had he run straight, to the right, or to the left? Noise echoed from my right, so that was the way I tried first.

I prayed again that I wouldn't get lost in the area. I moved along the uneven ground and that was when I spotted Grant. The inspector was on the ground and

Grant was standing over him. I wasn't sure what had happened, but I knew that Grant wasn't going to let the inspector get away.

As I neared the men, Grant called out, "Chloe, is that you?"

"Yes, it's me," I said.

Grant didn't turn around to look at me. "Can you call the police? My phone is in the truck on the seat."

"I've already called them." I'd barely finished my sentence when I heard sirens near us. "I'm going to tell them where you are."

"I think the inspector is willing to get up and meet the police. Isn't that right?" Grant asked him.

Porter nodded as he pushed to his feet. I didn't trust him though and I wanted the police to come and get him right away. When I reached the spot where I'd entered the tree line, the police saw me.

I pointed out Grant and the inspector. "The men are over there. The inspector ran me off the road and then he had an accident," I offered.

After the police spoke with Grant, they took the inspector away in handcuffs. I still wasn't sure what was going on with him.

Grant walked over and smiled. "Are you still okay?"

I nodded. "I'm much better now. I'm glad that wasn't any crazier than it had to be."

He stepped closer and wrapped his arms around me. I didn't push him away, although I still couldn't be with him. He couldn't just ignore what had happened. I knew what I'd seen. I broke free and pushed him away. He stepped back and stared at me. I saw the sadness in his eyes.

"You just can't hug me and expect that everything is okay now. It just won't work for us." I waved my hands.

"I know what you thought you saw today, but it's not what is going on," he said.

I stared at him. How could I trust him? How could I know that he was telling the truth?

"The woman you saw me with is my cousin's wife. She's married to my cousin Robert. Her mother is very sick and he's out of town. She came by to tell me and I offered her my support." Sincerity was evident out on his face.

Okay, now I felt stupid. But that didn't correct the past.

I looked down at my feet and then finally met his gaze. "I'm sorry. I didn't know, but what do you expect me to think after what happened?"

"What you think happened years ago never happened. You never gave me a chance to explain." Grant reached out and grasped my hand in his.

I stared at him. "What? You're trying to tell me after all these years that what I saw wasn't what really happened?"

"I wasn't with Debra. It was you I've always loved."

My stomach turned and I fought back tears in my eyes. I'd always loved Grant and this was almost more than I could handle.

Ty walked over and interrupted our conversation, which was fine with me because I needed time to think about what Grant had just told me. Why hadn't he told me before? Oh yeah, because I'd never given him that chance.

"We know what happened with Gina." Ty crossed his muscular arms across his chest casually as if he hadn't just arrested a psycho.

My eyes widened. "What do you mean?"

"The inspector was in love with Gina. He had Anna Louise kill her. He said he would kill Anna Louise's daughter if she didn't kill Gina."

"Is that why my uncle left?" I said.

He looked at me, confused. "What do you mean?"

"My uncle called me," I said.

"We haven't spoken with your uncle." Ty exchanged a look with Grant.

"He called me, but I didn't get a chance to figure out where he is."

Ty stared for a moment and then said, "If you hear from him again can you tell him to call us?"

I nodded. "I'll tell him. Did you ever find out why Porter wanted me out of town so badly?"

Ty met my gaze. "I suppose he wanted to avoid having to kill you."

A lump formed in my throat just thinking about how close I'd come to death.

Grant touched my arm. "Let's go back to my truck. We should get out of here."

"I need to tell the police about my accident and get my belongings out of the car."

"You'd packed your suitcase?" Disappointment filled his voice, sending a wave of regret through me.

I nodded. "Yes, I was headed to the airport and back to Arizona."

Grant looked away without responding. I figured I'd wait for him in the truck. If I'd hurt his feelings, I was sorry, but I never intended for that to happen.

When we were back in the truck, I said, "I should try to call my uncle. Do you mind if I use your phone now?"

He handed me the phone. "Not at all."

I pushed in my uncle's number and held my breath waiting for him to answer. I prayed that he would answer this time. After a few rings, he picked up.

"My phone died," I said. "Where are you?"

He hesitated. "I'm on my way back. I have to get you out of there. I didn't know you would go there. You need to get away."

"Why do you say that?" I asked.

"I never thought he would kill Gina." Emotion filled his voice.

"The inspector? How did you know that he had Gina killed?" I asked.

"Because he told me that he would do it. I found out what he was doing and he said he would kill Gina if I didn't leave. He told me not to have any contact with anyone from Belle Grove. Not my family or Gina. I just had to leave and not look back. I was trying to figure out what I was doing. He was taking bribes too. I found out about that. He was going to kill me, but now that Gina is gone, I have to face him." Anger thickened his words.

"Well, you don't have to worry about him now. The police just arrested him."

I explained the accidents and that the police knew that Anna Louise had killed Gina for the inspector. Now he just needed to tell them about the bribery.

My uncle said he would be back in just a few hours. What would I do until then? I had to stay and talk with him. After hanging up, I handed the phone back to Grant.

He squeezed my hand and smiled. "Is everything okay?"

I nodded. "He's on his way back. It'll be a couple hours."

We watched the police as they placed the inspector in the back seat of the police car. I explained to Grant about the bribery. "I guess that was the reason that my uncle couldn't get that building permit for his place."

"It doesn't surprise me," Grant said. "I knew Porter was bad when he first showed up in Belle Grove."

"I'm glad that he won't be around anymore."

We sat in silence for a moment watching the action unfolding in front of us. When the police drove off, it was time for us to make a decision. I couldn't exactly go anywhere now that I didn't have a car.

"What are you going to do?" Grant asked, breaking the silence.

I stared straight ahead and avoided his stare. I was going over what he had told me in my mind. I had been wrong all these years? Had we wasted time that we could have been together? I wasn't sure what to think, but I had to stop running and face this. If he was being truthful then I really wanted to find out. After all this time, I realized that I did believe him and that I should have given him a chance back then.

"Do you think there are bayous in Arizona?" I asked with a smile.

When I looked over at him, he was smiling. "I don't think so. If there had been I probably would have moved there years ago."

Now it was time for me to decide what I was going to do. Could I really stay in Belle Grove? I had nothing keeping me in Arizona. I didn't have to stay there. It would be a little sad to leave, since my place in Arizona was really nice, but the big problem with that was Grant wasn't there.

Grant reached out and touched my hand again. He probably knew that I was debating what to do in my mind. I met his gaze.

"I think you should stay," he said.

Grant reached over and pulled me close. His smell was intoxicating and his body felt right next to mine. How could I say no to him? With his gorgeous face looking at me and the way that he'd made me feel last night, I couldn't turn away from that now. I knew that he was waiting for my answer and I couldn't make him wait any longer. We had waited ten years to be together and I wanted to make up for lost time.

He took my hands in his and said, "So what do you say?"

I smiled at him and said, "I think I'll stay a while. I've gotten used to your smile and I don't think I can stay away from that."

"So you understand what I was trying to tell you? Debra and David are married now. They live in Baton Rouge. I was helping them get back together. You jumped to conclusions when you saw us hugging," he said.

I should have trusted him more than that.

I nodded. "I should have given you a chance. I wasted a lot of time by not trusting you."

He touched my cheek. "Well, that's all behind us now."

"I should have known that I wouldn't be able to stay away from Belle Grove forever." I wrapped my arms around Grant's waist.

"I'm glad you came home." I inched closer to his face.

Grant placed his lips on mine and kissed me like I'd never been kissed before. It felt so right and now I realized that romance wasn't just for my fictional characters. Now maybe I could have my real-life happily ever after.

I moaned beneath my breath. Grant settled his mouth on my lips.

The End

ABOUT ROSE PRESSEY

Rose Pressey is a USA Today bestselling author. She enjoys writing quirky and fun novels with a paranormal twist. The paranormal has always captured her interest. The thought of finding answers to the unexplained fascinates her.

When she's not writing about werewolves, vampires and every other supernatural creature, she loves eating cupcakes with sprinkles, reading, spending time with family, and listening to oldies from the fifties.

Rose suffers from Psoriatic Arthritis and has knee replacements. She might just set the world record for joint replacements. She's soon having her hips replaced, elbows, and at least one shoulder.

Rose lives in the beautiful commonwealth of Kentucky with her husband, son, and two sassy Chihuahuas.

Visit her online at:
http://www.rosepressey.com
http://www.facebook.com/rosepressey
http://www.twitter.com/rosepressey

Rose loves to hear from readers. You can email her at: rose@rosepressey.com

If you're interested in receiving information when a new Rose Pressey book is released, you can sign up for her newsletter at http://oi.vresp.com/?fid=cf78558c2a. Join her on Facebook for lots of fun and prizes.

Made in the USA
Lexington, KY
20 January 2017